AN ABSENT
MIND

ALSO BY ERIC RILL

Pinnacle of Deceit
The Innocent Traitor

AN ABSENT MIND

ERIC RILL

LAKE UNION
PUBLISHING

Text copyright © 2015 Eric Rill

Published by Lake Union, Seattle
www.apub.com

Amazon, the Amazon logo, and Lake Union are trademarks
of Amazon.com, Inc., or its affiliates.

ISBN-13: 9781477828540
ISBN-10: 1477828540

Cover design by Damonza

Library of Congress Control Number: 2014955243

Printed in the United States of America

In memory of Norman Rill (1913–1998), an Alzheimer's patient and wonderful father, and Lorraine Rill (1919–2007), an extraordinary caregiver and loving mother.

"I have lost myself."

In 1901, Mrs. Auguste D., a fifty-one-year-old woman from Frankfurt, Germany, displayed signs of cognitive and intellectual deterioration and became a patient of Dr. Alois Alzheimer. She died in 1906, and, after an autopsy, became the first person diagnosed with a form of dementia that became known as Alzheimer's.

PART ONE
THE DISCOVERY

SAUL

THE BEGINNING OF THE END

I was always considered a bit peculiar, so no one probably suspected anything until a dreary October afternoon when I removed my gray flannel trousers, opened the front door of my house, and ambled down the street. My wife, Monique, must have felt the damp breeze floating through the hallway into the kitchen, at least that's what she told the young resident at the hospital when she arrived at the emergency room.

I remember the astonished look of the bus driver when he refused to let me board, but don't remember crossing in front of a black Audi. A passerby told the policeman I danced blindly in front of the bus like a kid on his way to the playground, which is amusing considering I am a large man, seventy-one years old, with a belly that strains my belt.

My recollection is that the light had turned green, but to be honest, I really can't remember for sure. It could have been yellow, maybe even red. There have been several things that I haven't been sure about lately, like when I was standing in front of the stove, trying to figure out what to do with the pot in my hand. Then I remembered I had come in to make Monique a cup of tea, but I wasn't quite sure how to go about it.

At my last checkup a couple of years ago, Dr. Horowitz told me we all forget things as we get older, that our brains have a defined amount of space for memory, just like a computer, and we gradually get overloaded with "stuff." He said not to worry about it, because that would only make things worse. I took his advice, like always—after all, he had been our family doctor since . . . well, for a long time, that's for sure.

Anyway, the young resident at the hospital picked and prodded his way over my body. He stuck his flashlight in my eyes and then pulled out what looked like a silver hammer from his pocket and banged on my kneecaps. All that was starting to get me upset. But then he stopped and told me to get dressed, pointing to a brown paper bag that Monique had brought from the house.

As I fumbled with the buttons on my shirt, I heard him telling Monique how lucky I was to have only a few bumps and bruises. My blood pressure had shot up, he informed her, but that was normal given the circumstances. What circumstances? I wondered.

Then he motioned her toward the nurse's station, and they began whispering like wartime conspirators under the harsh fluorescent light. He kept jabbering, and she kept nodding. Finally, she walked back toward me, her eyes misty, dabbing at her mascara.

I had finished dressing and stood there holding the brown paper bag tightly under my arm. Monique pried the bag from me, opened it, and pulled out my gray flannel trousers.

MONIQUE
REALIZATION

Saul is sleeping soundly beside me now, his droopy ears hiding under the flat white hair that circles the lower part of his head. He has always been embarrassed about how large his ears are, but I think they're endearing—a slight imperfection in his almost perfect sense of style and looks.

Our marriage has lasted for almost forty-four years—forty-four years of *tsuris*—that's a Yiddish word for trouble or aggravation that Saul's mother taught me. In this case, it's been both.

I am French Canadian and was a practicing Catholic. Some of Saul's friends had married French Canadians, but they all converted to Judaism. There was no way that was going to happen to me, or so I thought at the time. When we told his mother there might not be a conversion, she said over her dead body would her son marry a *goy*.

We didn't have any Jews in the East End neighborhood of Montreal where I grew up. I never even saw one until I started working at a department store downtown. My uncle Alphonse, who worked in the Garment District, used to tell us stories of Jewish men with ringlet-like sideburns they never cut and women who wore funny wigs.

About a month after I started work, Saul came into the jewelry department and asked for a Star of David. I had no idea what he was talking about. Not that my English was bad; in fact, it was almost perfect, thanks to the fact that my mother sent me to a tutor after school on the little money she saved from her maid's salary. Saul smiled and explained it was like a cross, but for Jews. As I fumbled through the drawers under the counter, he looked down at me and asked if he could take me out for dinner the following night.

He showed up at my door on Rue Notre-Dame with a box of chocolates. The candy wasn't for me, but for my mother. I knew she would never approve of my going out with an older man, especially an English man. And I was certainly not going to tell her he was Jewish. But he did—in the first ten minutes. A half hour later, I had to drag him out the door, out of my mother's clutches.

You see, Saul was smoother than silk, like Frank Sinatra—a quality that has worked for and against him throughout his life. Sometimes it was just too easy for him to get what he wanted; sometimes he got it and wished he hadn't.

That's probably how he felt about me. He certainly chased after me, told me what I wanted to hear, what any young girl wants to hear from an older, powerful suitor. And he showered me with gifts.

One day we were walking downtown, and I admired a blouse in a shop window. He told me to wait outside, then barged through the door of the shop and came out with the same blouse in four different colors. Frankly, I would have been happier with a little more affection and fewer material possessions.

I should have realized early on that warmth would not be a cornerstone of our relationship, but I guess I was used to that from my childhood. I had no brothers or sisters, my father died when I was ten, and mother worked day and night to feed and clothe me.

We married in his synagogue after a two-year courtship, and after I converted to Judaism, but it didn't take long for things to go downhill. There were fights—I don't mean real fights—just constant bickering. But if you ask me if I love him, the answer would be, in a certain way, yes. And if I have been faithful, the answer is yes. And if he has been a good provider, the answer would be yes. Has he been a good father? One of the kids might say yes. Given everything, would I do it all over again? Maybe. Maybe not. But I made my choice years ago, and I am almost sixty-six and a grandmother.

In spite of it all, I thought we would grow old together. We had talked of moving out to Arizona to escape the damp winters because of his arthritis. But all that changed today.

The doctor on duty in the emergency room told me Saul should be tested for Alzheimer's. It's true he had been acting differently for several months—temper tantrums, hiding things around the house, telling the same stories over and over again, forgetting little things, being suspicious of me. I should have figured it out. And maybe I did and just didn't want to face it, hoping I was wrong. But if I'm honest with myself, you don't forget to put on your pants before you go out if you're normal.

Now, as I lie in our bed, my head resting beside his, listening to more of a purr than a snore, I fear that the rest of his life will be short and difficult. Mine may be long, but full of worry.

SAUL
THE FAMILY

Florence and Bernie came over today. I wish they wouldn't fuss over me like I were some kind of child or old fart. Maybe Bernie feels bad about getting upset with me last Thursday for wetting my pants and leaving a big stain on their good living room chair, although I explained to him that drinking all that water sometimes catches up with you—at least it caught up with me, and more than once.

Bernie is high-strung. You never know when he'll explode. He makes Mount Vesuvius look like a water fountain in a neighborhood park. I still can't figure out why Florence married him. Maybe because I told her not to. Well, I didn't exactly come out and say it, but she got the message. Next time I have a daughter, I'm going to tell her the opposite of what I think, and then she'll do it my way. Oh well, live and learn!

I haven't mentioned this yet, but we have another child, who is two years younger than Florence. His name is Joseph, but we've always called him Joey. Maybe that's because he still looks like a kid, with his long hair and dimples—and acts like one, too. He and Florence are as different as black and white.

Florence is an old soul—I'm sure she has been here on earth many times before this incarnation. I could tell that the first time I examined the inside of her hand when she was barely two weeks old. There were more lines crisscrossing her palm than there are on a Canadian football field. I say Canadian because a Canadian football field is ten yards longer than an American one and the playing field is also wider, although I don't recollect how many yards wider. But even to have more lines than an American football field on your hand at two weeks old proves my point.

I don't think Florence's pulse or blood pressure ever change. That's probably a good thing. Sometimes when I am boiling over, I just have to look over at her to find a peacefulness I could never discover on my own.

As for Joey, well, he is like a racehorse, always on the go. Need I say more?

Anyway, I got sidetracked. I wanted to finish up on Florence's Bernie. A real piece of work, as my father used to say. Oh yeah, my father—his name was Lawrence. He had the physique of a boxer, probably lightweight division. Just a little thicker than wiry, but not much. He had six-pack abs until he was almost seventy, and even then he still looked like the kind of guy who could eat nails for breakfast—big ones! Talk about Mount Vesuvius. He could blow like Mount Vesuvius and Mount Etna at the same time. And it would come from nowhere. Like the first bolt of lightning just before the sky blackens. Then just as quickly as he exploded, his famous smile would be plastered over his angular face.

Sorry, I was telling you about Bernie. He started hanging around our old house near the park just after Florence's graduation from high school, or was it before? Yes, it was before, because I can remember him sitting in the first row, blabbing away during the ceremony. Florence was the head of her class—you know the one I mean—the best one. And that was a big deal, at least to our family. But I guess not to Bernie.

I figured she would get over him and go on to the next one, like we all did at that age—well, almost all—but she didn't, and he became more of a fixture in our house than Roxy, the kids' mongrel dog. I say the kids', but I guess I was the true owner, since I bought her from the SPCA, walked her, fed her, and eventually buried her.

That was a fiasco. I came home one night and told the kids Roxy had died in her sleep. Actually, she was sick. I forget exactly what she had. The vet asked me if I wanted her put down. I figured it was the right thing to do, and it was. Unfortunately, I left the bill that listed the vet's services, including the cost of the stuff he used to put her to sleep, on my nightstand, and Joey found it. But that's another story for another time.

Florence and Bernie—sounds like some kind of bad television show—have two young children of their own. Nice kids, but the jury's still out on whether they will be like him or like her. Pray for the children!

Joey is a confirmed bachelor. Thirty-five, if I'm not mistaken, and into one thing—money. I swear, if there was a way to get rich from marketing the sweat that drips from my armpits after I wake up from one of those dreadful nightmares of falling into a never-ending black hole, he would be the one to do it. He has more scams going at one time than those guys—what do you call them? The ones who always seem to phone during dinner to sell you something. Anyway, you know who I mean.

Joey's had a few girlfriends, but they don't seem to last long. I liked the one with the curly blond hair, but he said she was a gold digger. At least she had big knockers. I like big knockers. Monique has big knockers.

I used to wonder whether Joey might be gay. You don't blow off a girl with knockers like that because she wants you to buy her a few trinkets. At least I wouldn't. But he doesn't look gay, whatever that means. I used to think being gay meant looking swishy, but Rock Hudson certainly didn't look swishy.

I hope Joey's not gay. That would be terrible. If I knew that for sure, I would probably never speak to him again. Although I remember back in college finding my girlfriend, Susan, in bed with her roommate, Karen. And I don't mean just in bed. I mean really in bed, if you know what I mean. And I kind of liked that. So maybe I would talk to him after all.

Joey was supposed to drop by this week, but he always has something going on, always some kind of excuse. He only comes by when he needs money, when his deals aren't going well. Monique doesn't get it, because she has never written a check in her life—wouldn't know how. God, if anything ever happens to me—although I can't imagine that, given the results of my last physical. Except for the memory bit, the doctor said I'm in great shape.

I sometimes forget where I park my car when I go to the mall. Florence always kids me that I have Mallzheimer's. But like I said, Dr. Horowitz told me it was normal to lose a little memory, although he did suggest I write things down. I have never written anything down—that's why I've had such a good memory all my life. So I'm way ahead of the game. Even if I lose a bit, I'll still have more than most men my age.

JOEY
THE VISIT

I went by to see Dad this morning. Frankly, after listening to Mom's stories, I was a bit concerned. But she's been known to be a little emotional. Well, that's kind of an understatement. In fact, sometimes she goes off the deep end for the most ridiculous reasons. I remember coming home from school in the eighth grade with a split lip. She was on the phone to the principal, the police, and the doctor before I even finished telling her what had happened. So I always have to take her "fragility," shall we say, into account before jumping to conclusions.

According to her, Dad is really losing it. She said he's forgetful, introverted, and submissive. I don't know about the forgetful part. I have noticed a few things, but nothing that seemed really worrisome. After all, he is in his seventies. But my dad has never been, and wouldn't know how to be, introverted or submissive. Those are traits I would save for Mom. In fact, Dad has always been the rock of the family—the disciplinarian, the provider, the powerhouse.

I haven't been over to the house for a while, what with getting this distributorship thing going. I've got the rights for Canada for this rejuvenating cream. It's got a special herb that they grow in the highlands of Panama, as well as a patented blend of ingredients which, unfortunately, I can't share with you, as I signed a confidentiality agreement.

In today's world, everyone is so vain, and they all want to look younger. So this will be a slam dunk. Dad thinks it's a pyramid scheme and said he doesn't even want to hear about it. He said I'll get busted one day, and that will ruin my reputation. My bet is it's his reputation he's worried about. But he'd never admit that, and I learned a long time ago that it's not worth arguing with him, because I can never win.

When I arrived, he was sitting in front of the television set, patting his beloved collie. Ever since he bought that dog a few years ago, it's like he has three kids, and let me assure you, Dugin is the favorite. Anyway, I yelled out, "Yo Pops," like I always do, but the only one who acknowledged my presence was Dugin, and that was only with a lazy wag of his tail.

Mom heard the door slam and came in from the kitchen. She gave me one of her pained looks and pointed to Dad, motioning with her hand for me to move over to the couch.

I sat down opposite him and said again, "Yo Pops." He looked away from the television and gave me a smile. "Hi, Son, what's happening?" he asked. I told him how my ceiling had almost collapsed from a water leak in the upstairs apartment. He responded, "Great, just great!" Then he was back, staring at the television again. I looked over at Mom. She just shrugged her shoulders and headed back into the kitchen with her *I told you so* look.

So there we were: the tough, son of a bitch father and the ne'er-do-well son, sitting alone in the living room, a restless silence filling the air. Not very different from when I lived at home, before I moved out to go to university.

I tried to pull his attention away from the television, but with no success. So I finally got up and turned it off. He asked me why

13

I had done that. I told him I'd come over to talk to him. Again he said, "That's great, just great!" I tried again to engage him in conversation, but he just sat there stroking Dugin. And then two minutes later, he got up and walked out of the room, like I didn't even exist.

Now I'm worried about him. This is not normal behavior, not for him, not for anybody. When Mom told me about the incident with his pants last month, my first reaction was that he probably had a few too many. He's certainly been known to do that. But seeing him today, I don't think that's the case. I'm going to give Florence a jingle tonight.

FLORENCE
THE TELEPHONE CALL

Joey called me earlier. I have never heard him so upset. He started to lash out at me, asking why I hadn't told him how serious things were with Father. That was all I needed to hear. "How dare you talk to me like that?" I exploded. "I have been telling you that I've noticed there was something wrong with him for some time. And you didn't even bother going over to see for yourself, or just to spend time with him. And why is it always my responsibility, not only to do everything but to do it to your specifications, and on your timing? I'm not on your payroll, damn it!"

I was actually quite proud of myself for blowing off steam with Joey. That's not my typical modus operandi. I am usually the one who sits there like a good little girl and takes whatever is shoveled my way, whether it be from my mother, my father, my husband, or Joey. But lately, it has been too much for me. I'm like a soup pot that starts frothing and then floods over onto the stovetop.

I'm at the house more often than usual now. It's bad enough that Father's got, at least in my opinion, the beginnings of some kind of dementia. But I can never get Mother to discuss it. And, of course, I could never steal any of Joey's precious time for him to check it out himself. I feel I am totally alone.

Father and I still go for a walk on most weekends. It's always been our time together. We ramble down the hill toward the park and just hang around or go over to the dog run. Some days he is just like the father I remember; other days aren't so good. I'm not implying that his life is over or anything like that. It's just that there are those occasions, clearly not all the time, when he gets a bit strange, or quiet, or disoriented. But just when I begin to question his behavior, he's back to his same old self.

After I finished telling Joey off, he quieted down rather quickly. I think he was as taken aback as I was by my harangue. In fact, he apologized for not being more available and promised he would do whatever it took from now on to help all of us deal with this. My mouth was agape. I can't remember him ever doing anything where there wasn't an angle, and frankly, I'm not sure it will be any different this time.

SAUL
LOST FREEDOM

The Gestapo showed up today in their winter coats and boots—Joey, Bernie, and Florence. Monique and I were pretty astute naming her, or is it that she has spent a lot of her young life trying to live up to the moniker we bestowed on her? Florence, as in Florence Nightingale, but by now I'm sure you figured out what I meant, has been at more bedsides than a paid executioner at hangings. And she does it for free and generally brings some goodies to boot. If you ever have to be sick, try to have a daughter like mine!

I asked her once why she didn't become a nurse; that was before a question like that became sexist. Now we'd have to ask why she didn't become a doctor. Regardless, the answer would have been the same. She gets sick at the sight of blood.

I used to wonder whether she inquired as to the type of illness before committing to visit a relative, friend, acquaintance, or fellow employee—she's an accountant by trade, like my father was, but she's a damn good one. If the truth be told, I tried to talk her out of it, not because she lacked the skills, but I just had trouble thinking of her in the same profession as my father. He seems to haunt me even from six feet under.

But I'm getting sidetracked again. So I'm sitting in the living room of our bungalow on Oakland Avenue. It's nothing great, considering the other houses in the neighborhood. Westmount is the fancy borough of Montreal. It used to be a fancy city, but they did something to make it a borough, some kind of vote or something, although I'm not exactly sure I understood what it was. But now I've heard it may be a city again. Whatever. It really is of no importance. At least not to me.

Our house sits at the end of a cul-de-sac, a dead end in most other cities, but Montreal is almost all French, so they like these French expressions. I'm an Anglo. That's what they say to let others know I'm English-speaking. They use that word a lot and then break it down into Jews and Gentiles. And then there's what they call allophones—that means everyone else, like the Italians, Greeks, and the rest of them. And then there are the Gentiles, like Monique, who convert to Judaism. It's all really quite confusing.

I was describing our house. It sits on a *Father Knows Best* kind of street and is quite comfortable. We've been here since just before Monique gave birth to Joey.

That brings me back to the Nazis who showed up this afternoon. They were on a mission—to destroy my life! They huddled around me, all of them. It felt like when the Indians surrounded the wagons in the movies I went to see as a kid in Ontario. No, I didn't ever live in Ontario, but, you see, they had a big fire in a movie theater in Montreal back then, and the provincial government, in its infinite wisdom, banned kids under sixteen from going to the movies. So my mother, oh yeah, sorry about that—her name was Hannah, right out of the Bible. Anyway, Mother would pack us up, and we would visit my aunt Riva and uncle Sydney in Cornwall, just over the Quebec border. I would spend all day, from when the movie house opened in the morning until I had to be back for dinner, watching Gene Autry and other actors and actresses fighting, kissing, arguing, and riding through the brush.

Sometimes the same movie would play four times before I had to leave. My buddies and I would hide in the bathroom when the usher came in between shows, and then sneak back in. If there were teenagers necking, we would sit behind them and make funny sounds; at least I thought they were funny, until one of them gave me a walloping shiner. Father grounded me for a week. They didn't call it grounding then; it was called room time.

Back to Hitler's finest. They squeezed onto the sofa by the fireplace, all except Joey, who can't sit for more than the time it takes him to gulp down a milk shake. I often wonder what happens when he's in the bathroom. With his attention span, he probably can't sit still until it's time to reach for the toilet paper.

Florence was the first to speak. No doubt prodded by the others, because they know I think hers is the voice of reason. But not today. She said that they had all discussed it. She said it with hooded eyes and a pained expression. She just kept beating around the bush, never saying what the "it" was. Then Joey butted in, blabbering something about me maybe killing someone. Now, I know Dr. Horowitz said my memory is not what it was, but I can't for the life of me remember coming close to murdering anyone. I mean, yes, there were times when someone in the room may have been the recipient of one of my Reimer stares. They call it the Reimer stare because, as Monique once said, "That stare of yours can make mere mortals quiver in their boots." And because my name is Saul Reimer.

Florence moved over beside me and started to massage my shoulders as Joey continued his rant. He said I was getting old and my driving was becoming defensive. I was driving too slowly, and that was dangerous. Christ! All I ever heard for the last umpteen years was how I was a speed demon, and how dangerous *that* was. Now the troops had advanced into my own living room and were telling me I drive like a tortoise. Worse, the punishment was to take my car away from me.

Take my car? How was I going to get around? They said—well, actually it was Joey who said he would give me taxi vouchers—with my own money, of course. All I had to do was sign them. I could go anywhere. I asked if I could go to New York. Joey smiled. Joey doesn't smile very often. Too bad he wasted it on such an idiotic statement. I knew he wasn't going to let me go to New York. I would be lucky if he let me take a cab downtown.

I folded my arms across my chest and said I was not going to give him the keys and that I would continue driving. Joey told me about the eighty-year-old man in California who killed ten people, including two children. I told him I am not eighty and I am a good driver. He said it wouldn't be fair to kill a child. I told him I wasn't planning on it, although I must admit I was starting to think about how to get rid of one of my own—and it wasn't Florence I had in mind.

I know this all started after the incident when I forgot my pants. And I told Joey that I wouldn't forget to put my trousers on again—never, ever. But Joey said the matter was closed. The others in his division mumbled under their breath, nodded their heads, and offered up sad but resolute expressions. Then Joey said it was best this way. Best for whom?

MONIQUE
SADNESS

Unfortunately, it takes forever to get a doctor's appointment here in Quebec because of the socialized medical system, but I finally got one for Saul to see Dr. Horowitz three weeks after I first called. Saul has been down in the dumps, but the doctor said that was normal. Actually, he said Saul was less depressed than most early Alzheimer's patients, although he made it very clear that he was only a general practitioner and that we should go and see someone who specializes in that field to get a firm diagnosis. He gave me a referral to Dr. Yves Tremblay. I made the appointment—this time, a two-month wait!

Saul is so different now. Here was a man who roared at his own gags no matter how bad they were, someone who had so much energy, we all joked that he must be on drugs. And now he seems withdrawn, not wanting to participate in any activities except sitting in front of the television with a blank look in his eyes. The only good thing is that he doesn't click the remote over and over anymore. That used to drive me crazy.

The other night, he got up while we were playing gin and threw his cards on the table, saying he had no interest in playing any longer. When I asked him why, he said the game was for imbeciles. But I could tell he was becoming frustrated because he couldn't remember all the rules and didn't want me to know. I told him I would help him with his hand. Then he really got angry and stormed out of the room. Minutes later, he was back, dragging a sheet from the linen closet. When I asked him what he was doing, he just stared at me.

Today, everyone was there to give Joey support as he told Saul that he shouldn't drive anymore. Joey told us it was going to be like taking a man's penis away. Sometimes, for an educated young man, he has a foul mouth.

This is going to make our lives more difficult, because I never learned to drive. I think Saul's driving is okay, maybe a little slow, certainly better than the kids who speed around Mount Royal in their fancy cars. But Joey said it was too dangerous, and the others agreed.

Saul didn't take it well. I could see him fuming under his stiff smile. A few minutes after they left, he collapsed onto the sofa by the window and started sobbing—the first time I ever actually saw him break down. Once, after Florence was born, I heard him crying through the bathroom door. Those were tears of happiness.

I walked over to the sofa and sat down beside him. He took my hand and held it to his wet face. I started to weep. He asked what was wrong. I told him it hurt me that he was so sad. Suddenly, his tears stopped. He threw my arm off his chest and left the room.

I never know what to expect anymore. But I guess that's a minor problem compared to what he's going through. I can't even imagine the anguish he must be feeling, knowing he will morph into someone I no longer know, and someone who does not know me. But I will be by his side, giving him whatever support I can—that's the least I can do after so many years of marriage.

SAUL
DAY OF RECKONING

The road wound endlessly through the flower-covered grounds of Roxboro Hospital. I thought Monique had tricked me. She told me we were going to see Dr. Tremblay, who is considered the guru for Alzheimer's in Canada, and maybe the world. She said Dr. Horowitz is not an expert, and so only someone like Dr. Tremblay would really know. I was worried, not so much about maybe having Alzheimer's, but that she was going to have me committed. You see, Roxboro is a mental hospital. She assured me that Dr. Tremblay's office was not part of the hospital; rather, he just rented office space there. I figured maybe this was a conspiracy being perpetrated by Monique to get me out of the way so she could marry that guy who sings those romantic songs on television.

I had been to Roxboro only once, many years ago, and that was to visit one of my former associates from Legrand et Fils, the paper company I managed. His name was Jean-Paul something or other. A nice guy, but nuts! I figured that out my first day on the job, when he started chanting like he was a French-Canadian rabbi or something. Grand-Luc Legrand, the owner, so called not because of a stout girth, but, rather, as a tribute to his incredible height, didn't figure it out for a few years, or maybe he didn't want to know. But when Jean-Paul set fire to a huge pile of paper in front of him and the floor supervisor, practically blowing up the building, even he had to acknowledge it. Jean-Paul was committed the next day.

Roxboro is typical of the mental hospitals you see in the movies— gray, dank, and scary—not somewhere I would like to spend any meaningful time, that's for sure. I would make quite a scene if they tried to get me committed there. That you can count on.

But it turned out Monique was telling me the truth. The office was in a small house by the back entrance of the hospital, probably a caretaker's house years ago. I knew she was right when I spotted the brass plaque with Dr. Tremblay's name on it on the front door. We waited in the empty anteroom until he bounded up the stairs, introduced himself, and led the way down to a large room in the basement.

Dr. Tremblay pointed to a chair in front of his desk, and I sat down beside Monique. He began asking her questions—like if I misplaced things. Well, of course I misplace things; everyone does. And that's all she had to tell him. But no, she pulled out a wad of paper and told him a whole bunch of things—most of which I am sure were lies.

He asked Monique if I sometimes got lost. She told him how I had left the house to get a newspaper and was gone for hours. And how Westmount security called her to come and get me down at the station near City Hall, or whatever they call it now. I jumped in and reminded her that they were the banana police. The doctor didn't know what banana police are, so I figured maybe he had a problem.

Monique explained that they are Westmount security officers who drive these yellow jeeps and aren't really police, but give parking tickets and call the real police if there is a serious problem. He nodded like he really knew that, but I doubt it.

Then she told him about the incident with my trousers. I don't know what happened, but I watched myself jump up from my seat and grab her by the shoulders. He was on our side of his big desk before you could say "yikes"—that's what I used to say when I was a kid: "yikes."

Next thing I knew, I was back in my seat, and the doctor was between Monique and me, leaning against the desk and continuing his interrogation. He asked Monique if I had lost interest in the things I used to love to do. She said I used to love the outdoors, tennis, and golf, but now all I do is stay in the den and watch television. Now that may be true, but at my age, what does she want me to do, take up bungee jumping?

The doctor smiled at me as he returned to his desk. I guess that was to reassure me or something. Then he started asking me all kinds of foolish questions. Like what floor we were on. I told him we were in the basement, but you would think he would have known that. Then he asked me who the president of the United States was. That one, I didn't know, but I told him there are probably some Americans who wouldn't get that one, either. He smiled. Then he asked me what the day and date were. I knew it was Monday because Monique hadn't gone to her volunteer thing yesterday, but the date? "No," I mumbled, "I don't know the date."

"What's my name?" he asked. I explained that I didn't want to be rude, but I meet so many people. He nodded and smiled again.

The doctor then asked me to count backward from one hundred by sevens.

"Ninety-three," I said quickly. Ninety-three minus seven? I thought for a minute about that one as I closed my eyes. "Eighty-six," I ventured. He nodded his head. Now I was on a roll. Eighty-six minus seven? I closed my eyes again, but it just wouldn't come. I figured I might as well guess. "Seventy-something . . . seventy-five?" I finally mumbled. He said something about my doing fine and that

I could stop. I protested that I could get the next one right, but my mind went blank.

Then he held up some pictures of things and asked me what they were. The first two were easy, a flower and a house. I missed the next one, which he told me was a volcano, and I missed the one after that. Actually, I knew it, but I just couldn't find the word. He said it was a funnel. After a few more pictures, some of which I identified, he gave me a piece of paper with some lines on it. It kind of looked like a house. He asked me to draw it. I did the best I could, but I knew it wasn't very good. I told him I'd never been very artistic.

Then he gave me another piece of paper with a circle and the number twelve at the top. He told me to fill in the other numbers of the clock and make the hands show ten to eleven. It didn't look like a clock then, or after I'd scribbled on it.

After that, he had me walk across the room in some funny way. I did what he said and I did it well, because I saw him put a check mark in a box on his sheet. Then he pulled some tubes out of a drawer and asked me to sniff them and tell him what they smelled like. Some of them didn't smell at all, I told him. He put an *x*, not a check mark, this time.

The doctor turned to me and asked me my birth date. By now I was tired, but I really wanted to show him I knew it. "February," I said. "February the tenth."

Monique nodded like I was right. Well, of course I was right. Everyone knows their birthday.

"What year?" he asked.

My face flushed. After a moment, I shook my head and told him I wasn't quite sure.

Then the doctor wanted to know if I remembered what we first talked about when we arrived at his office.

"What do you mean?" I said.

He asked me to describe our earlier conversation. I told him I remembered some of it. "Good," he replied. "Tell me."

It seemed like he had rattled off so many things so quickly. They all blurred into something in my brain that I couldn't make out. I was having trouble even getting the words out—and to be frank, I wasn't sure which words I wanted to come out. He stood there in front of me, leaning back against his desk, patiently waiting for my response. I glanced over at Monique. Her mascara was running.

MONIQUE
CONFIRMATION

I guess I already knew it. But when a man in a white coat with more diplomas on his wall than there are flowers on my bedroom wallpaper confirmed Dr. Horowitz's diagnosis that Saul has Alzheimer's, it felt like they might as well have been closing the lid of his coffin.

Saul kept glancing over at me for help when he didn't know the answers to Dr. Tremblay's questions. I looked over at his stooped shoulders and tired face. This was not the man I married. Not the man whose booming voice frightened those around him. Not the man who was so tough on the children. All of that is gone. Now he seems more like my child than my husband. But I don't need another child. I need a husband.

I could tell he was embarrassed. I wanted to help him with the answers, if only to preserve his dignity. That is one of the few things he has left, but Alzheimer's will rob him of that soon enough.

After the examination, Dr. Tremblay asked Saul to wait in the anteroom so he could talk to me. Saul didn't budge. My first thought was that he was just being stubborn, not one of his best traits. Then I realized that he didn't understand the doctor's request. The same way he didn't understand when the doctor had pulled a piece of paper out of his drawer and held it up. The words *Close your eyes* were printed on it in block letters. Saul looked at the paper as if it were blank. Finally, the doctor asked him if he knew what it meant. Saul said yes, but he continued to stare straight ahead. The doctor glanced over at me with a reassuring look and put the paper back in its place.

Dr. Tremblay stood up and asked Saul to go outside with him. Saul looked over at me. I nodded. Then the doctor followed him out to the waiting room, returning alone a few moments later.

He cleared his throat—not once, but twice—and then stated Saul had Alzheimer's and that it was still in what he called the early to moderate stage. He said there might be good days, when Saul was more or less lucid, others when he would appear to be lucid but drift off, and just plain bad days.

"The bottom line," he explained, "is that it may sometimes be hard for you to understand where Saul is in this quickly changing landscape." Those were his exact words.

He said it wouldn't be too long until it got worse. I asked him what that meant. He cleared his throat again and told me that Saul had anomia. He said that meant when Saul couldn't find the word he wanted, he would describe characteristics of the word—like calling a toothbrush a tooth cleaner, or a key a door opener.

He said Saul's test scores showed what was typical at this stage—to leave sentences unfinished, repeat phrases, use words that mean nothing, like "That's cool" or "You're right." And it's also normal at this stage to forget how to make sentences, have less interest in conversation, and not understand simple commands.

I asked him what happens in the final stage. He looked down at the floor and said something like, "Let's take this one step at a time." I told him I wanted to know now. He said he had another patient in the anteroom and suggested it would be better for me to see a counselor at the Alzheimer's Society. Could it be that bad that even a doctor was uncomfortable discussing it?

SAUL
GROUNDHOG DAY

There was this movie, *Groundhog Day*, with some comic and a gorgeous actress with dark, curly hair who is always on those TV commercials for some shampoo. God, I wish I could think of the name—no, not his—hers. She was a real piece!

As I recollect, and forgive me if I don't get it quite right, this weather reporter would keep going through the same stuff day after day. I remember thinking at the time, Hey, that wouldn't be so bad if I could spend every day with her. Well, it didn't quite work out that way, did it?

I mean, I often catch myself doing the same thing over and over, and even if I don't realize it, I'm sure I do repeat stuff, but the only one I see every day is Monique. Now, I'm not saying she's an eyesore. In fact, in her day she was quite something. Those knockers could stand up to anyone's back then. Today, they don't stand up at all—gee, I should be a comic! But let's face it: she's no beauty, certainly not today.

So I end up in a B-movie version of *Groundhog Day*. One that will never end, until the end. And by then, maybe it won't matter if that actress is there or not. I guess at least with Monique, I know she'll be there. That actress might have blown me off for another guy and not even have come to my funeral.

DR. TREMBLAY
DEATH SENTENCE

I have specialized in dementia for over thirty years and have seen thousands of probable Alzheimer's cases. I say probable, because so far, absent a brain biopsy, we haven't had sufficient tools to state with absolute certainty that a person has Alzheimer's. Although there is a study that analyzes spinal fluid for amyloid beta, a protein fragment that forms plaque in the brain, and tau, a protein that leaks out of dying nerve cells in the brain. It seems that all the subjects in the study who had Alzheimer's had the plaque, and all of those with mild cognitive impairment who had the plaque went on to develop Alzheimer's within five years.

There are also noninvasive tests like positron emission tomography, which can detect a decrease in glucose consumption; electroencephalograms, which examine a slowing of the alpha rhythm; and magnetic resonance imaging, which can identify a decrease in volume in the hippocampus, where Alzheimer's always starts. But these tests usually only reinforce our preliminary findings on assessments like the mini mental state examination or the Buschke selective reminding test.

I performed several tests on Mr. Reimer. It was quite clear to me, even before he scored only seventeen out of thirty on the MMSE—a score of twenty-four or higher indicates some degree of normality, but in point of fact, most fully functioning people would have a near-perfect score—that he was in the early stage and perhaps close to the middle stage of Alzheimer's. He did no better on the clock test or the trail-making test.

I don't want to get technical with you here, but it is important that you have at least some comprehension about how Alzheimer's affects the brain, so that you can understand what happens to people like Mr. Reimer. I will try to explain it to you in concise layman's language, although we doctors seem to have difficulty parsing convoluted medical terms.

Alzheimer's is characterized by the formation of cellular debris in the form of plaques and tangles. The plaques float between the neurons, while the tangles attack the neurons from inside the cell membranes. But regardless of how they go about their destruction, they achieve the same result, preventing the neurons from communicating with one another. As clumps of neurons die, specific functions such as short-term memory, spatial relationships, reasoning, and eventually things like muscle coordination, and even swallowing, are affected. The result is always death.

One of the sad things about this horrible disease is the time line. On average—and I say on average, because it's different for everyone—it takes about six to ten years for the disease to run its course. I have seen it take a much shorter time in patients with early-onset Alzheimer's, where the disease starts when the person is in his forties or fifties—but that's usually a specific inherited gene and not what Mr. Reimer has—to over twenty years in rare cases.

Mr. Reimer and his wife just left my office. He already has some anomia—difficulty in finding the right word, but is capable of circumlocution—talking around the word that can't be recalled.

He seems to have only the beginnings of agnosia. What I mean by that is he can still recognize most objects and know what they're for. For instance, he knew what to do with the pen he used to draw on one of the assignments I gave him. And he still recognizes those around him. And as for apraxia, spatial relationships, and motor skills, he had only a little trouble, which is normal in the earlier part of the disease.

I ordered a computer scan of the brain, as well as some blood tests for Mr. Reimer as a complement to a clinical evaluation. The results of the latter will give me a fairly accurate depiction of where he fits on the one-to-seven Reisberg Scale. Number three represents minimal cognitive dysfunction. By the time patients get to number seven, they are usually in a care facility, unable to function at all, even to lift their heads or open their eyes for any meaningful period of time.

Assuming the tests confirm my preliminary diagnosis, I will start him on medication, which will not slow down the disease but will help alleviate the symptoms for at least a few months, or maybe even a year or two, giving him a better quality of life during that time.

I will also schedule an appointment with Mr. Reimer's wife, the primary caregiver, not only to search out more information on the progress of her husband's disease, but also to evaluate her own health and coping skills. She told me she has a history of heart problems, high blood pressure, and elevated cholesterol. Taking care of her husband will put a lot of stress on Mrs. Reimer, so we have to be especially careful.

I spend more than half my time doing research into possible cures, but I know deep down that any significant discovery that would eradicate this horrific disease is years away. That is too many years to stave off the death sentence that I pronounced on Mr. Reimer today.

SAUL
THE LYNCH PARTY

The usual suspects were once again gathered at our house. This was to be a family council meeting, they told me, but I knew what it really was—a lynch party for one Saul Reimer.

Moses, in the guise of my daughter, Florence, spoke first. She informed the others that her father—that would be me—had been diagnosed with Alzheimer's by the preeminent doctor in the field. Joey asked if they should get a second opinion. Everyone looked at Monique. Why, I don't know. Maybe they had a hunch that Monique and Dr. Tremblay were friends, maybe more than friends. She said another opinion wouldn't be necessary, that Dr. Tremblay had done all of the tests and that it was clear that the diagnosis was correct. I don't know if it was, but I guess one consolation is that I'm not going to be committed to Roxboro!

Monique explained to the others that the doctor had told her sometimes my brain stalls. My brain stalls—I like that one. I'll try to remember it. Anyway, he told her to get me one of those yellow pads so she can make lists of what I have to do every day, things like taking the pills he's prescribed, brushing my teeth, dressing, having breakfast, and making sure not to leave the stove on. I thought that was pretty silly. Yes, I have forgotten a few things, maybe more than a few, but I am still normal—more or less.

I told them I still remembered a lot from a long time ago. Like when Harry Potash had tried to steal Sharon Wertheimer from me in the fifth grade, and how I had decked him in the school yard. That had cost me a week of recesses, but it was well worth it!

I had always been a tough guy. In fact, I got suspended for a brawl in the tenth grade. Ian Coulter was the resident bully and self-appointed chief anti-Semite of the school. Coulter was picking a fight with Buddy Rubin, the class weakling. He grabbed Buddy's thick glasses from his pointed nose, made a show of dropping them in almost slow motion to the icy sidewalk, and then slammed his heel down, crushing them. I could live with that, because you can't be everyone's protector. But then Coulter crossed the line. He called Buddy a kike.

Coulter missed the rest of the term because of a dislocated jaw and a broken arm, and it was only March. I was suspended for a month. That didn't sit well with Larry—I called my father Larry sometimes because he seemed to like it. And for some strange reason, it made me feel closer to him, like we were buddies. Anyway, Larry went apeshit, and I didn't see daylight on the weekends till summer vacation.

So I told the people who had taken over my living room that I could remember lots of things.

Monique put her hand on my shoulder and said, "Do you remember what Dr. Tremblay told us about how it's normal for Alzheimer's patients to have good long-term memory but lose short-term memory?"

"No," I said, "I don't remember." But my best guess is, so far at least, that I only have Sometimer's, not Alzheimer's.

JOEY
LOOKING BACK

There were so many clues, but I guess it's kind of like vegetable soup. If you have one piece of carrot in a broth, it's not vegetable soup. If you add some celery and beets, it's probably not, either. So when is it? There is no set amount or type of vegetables when one can definitively say that it's vegetable soup. And I think it's the same with Alzheimer's. It just starts to germinate and suddenly one day it's the real McCoy.

I remember when I met Dad for lunch downtown last year. He looked fine and was quite talkative. When I said good-bye outside the restaurant, he seemed at a bit of a loss.

He glanced up and down the street and finally said with a sheepish grin, "Son, I forget where I parked the car."

I thought to myself that was no big deal. But when I asked him where he thought it might be, the question elicited only a blank look and a shrug of his shoulders.

"You have no idea?" I asked.

He told me that he had been preoccupied with an audit by Revenue Canada. Who could argue with that? If I were undergoing a tax audit, I might very well forget where I'd parked my car—or, for that matter, if I even owned one! Anyhow, I suggested we start walking around and looking—and there it was—just across the street, half a block away.

The real kicker, and I can't believe it didn't set off alarm bells in my head, was when he called me up and asked me to go to a hockey game. I love hockey, especially the Montreal Canadiens, and we hadn't been to a game together in over twenty-five years—and then only after I practically got on my knees and begged him to take me for my tenth birthday.

We arrived at the Bell Centre a half hour early. I asked Dad for the tickets as we approached the entrance. He shuffled through the pockets of his overcoat and then his pants. By the pained expression on his face, I knew we had a problem—and we did. He had forgotten the tickets and said he had no idea where he had put them.

I could see he was getting agitated, so I said, "Pops, no problem; I'll just buy a couple." The box office was sold out, so I finally had to purchase seats from a scalper—what a rip-off! Luckily, I had been to the bank that day, because Dad had also forgotten his wallet.

The first period was pretty slow, a rarity when the Canadiens play the Maple Leafs. So I figured that Dad was just bored and it wasn't his thing. But it was almost as if he weren't in the arena. During the first intermission, he almost tripped twice going down the stairs. He said he didn't need to go to the men's room during the second intermission, even though I could tell by his wincing and crossing and uncrossing his legs that he probably had a full bladder.

While waiting for the third period to begin, he told me he had been toying with the idea of making a large contribution to some Catholic charity that had called to solicit a donation. He said the woman told him that they did a lot of good in the community. He said it just like he might have been commenting on the weather. Now, my father isn't the most religious Jew in the world, but to give his money to a Catholic organization? The Combined Jewish

Appeal finds it hard enough to extract a few dollars from him every year. Anyway, at the time I figured he was kidding. Now I'm not so sure.

PART TWO
COPING

SAUL
THE FACADE

It's been almost two years since they told me how sick and useless I was. I am able to keep it more or less together most days. And I stress days, because by dinnertime my mind is exhausted. I never knew you could have an exhausted mind, but I do now. The sheer weight of having to pretend I am normal all day for my friends, or the store clerks, feels like a boulder around my neck. What happens toward sundown is like when you hear the snap, crackle, and pop when the transistors in your old television go bad. Everything numbs and becomes foggy. Sights, sounds, and smells meld into a ball and explode toward the sky. It's as if I'm not the same person I was when I got up.

As of now anyway, I can see everything I want to say as clear as ice. It's right there on a blackboard in front of me, spelled out perfectly. But then to actually say what's written on the blackboard isn't always a piece of cake. Sometimes it's easy, like it is right now. I know what I'm saying to you is coherent and that my vocabulary is correct—but that could suddenly change and become difficult, sometimes impossible.

In the morning, I can be happy—well, maybe not happy, but not feeling sorry for myself. It's different by lunch—if I remember to eat, and I generally do because it's on my list, although I have been known to leave my pad somewhere and not be able to find it; if that happens, Monique usually reminds me. At least I think she does. Regardless, by lunchtime things generally start to go downhill.

Today, while I was sitting in my easy chair, she bent down to kiss me and brought her hand quickly to her mouth.

"Whew," she said, or something like that. "You didn't brush your teeth. Why did you check it off?"

I didn't bother answering, not because she was interrupting my soap opera—I really wasn't focusing anyway—but because I didn't know the answer. Maybe I didn't check the toothbrush to see if it was wet or dry, like I've been doing. Then she scolded me, like it was my fault. First they tell you you're sick because you can't remember anything and then they give you hell for not remembering.

The doorbell rang, and Monique disappeared for a minute, reappearing with Arthur Winslow in tow. I was standing there with the telephone receiver in my hand. Monique took it from me and put it back in the cradle.

Arthur was in high school with me and was actually the one who squealed to the principal that I was the one who decked Ian Coulter. Coulter, even though one of the great anti-Semites of all time, lived by a code of honor and wouldn't have turned me in, but Arthur did, and I understand why. You see, Arthur was the goody-goody of the class. He would have turned in his own mother if she had done something wrong. But other than squealing on me, he was a true and trusted friend.

Arthur lives down the street—at least I think he still does—and faithfully drops in to see me. Sometimes I think he has nothing else to do. I can't tell if he has missed any days visiting, or, if so, how many, but that doesn't matter now. What I do know is he cares, and I hope he keeps coming, even if I don't recognize him one day.

I already know that there will come a time when I won't know him, or people like Bernie. Frankly, I don't give a damn if I don't recognize Bernie—in fact, that could be the Lord's gift to me, something to make up for what lies ahead. What does bother me—in fact, scares the hell out of me—is not recognizing the kids. As inconceivable as that seems, they say it will happen as sure as night follows day. Who, you may ask, are *they*? I remember when I was a kid, my grandmother would always quote the almighty *they*. I would ask her, "Who are *they*, Granny?" She would always answer, "You know, *they*." I think maybe she had Alzheimer's!

SAUL
LOVE LETTERS

I've never been the sappy type and, believe me, I'm not now. But I know I am getting to the point where I soon will not be able to communicate meaningfully with anyone. That wouldn't be so terrible, except that I don't want to miss the chance to let the kids know how I feel about them.

In the best of circumstances, I can't talk about anything involving emotion. That's a given, and one that wouldn't have changed even if I hadn't gotten the big A. But I have never been faced with extinction before. It would be pretty shitty leaving this place without letting Florence and Joey know I love them. Yes, Monique, too, but she sort of knows. I mean, we've had good and bad. I don't think it's one of those soul mate kind of unions, but it isn't terrible, either. My guess is she probably feels the same way. We have few things in common, and except for when we would travel, we would always be arguing. I don't know what it was about the travel that worked out that way, but there you have it.

As for the kids, they know I'm not demonstrative. Maybe even a cranky pain in the ass. I hope they know how much I care, but in reality, how can they when I don't reach out to them, and when they reach out to me, I slink back into my cocoon? Well, maybe slink is the wrong word, but you get the drift—I just don't like to talk mush.

Even if I were to go today, and they were here, I probably wouldn't be able to look them in the eye and tell them I love them and how privileged I am to be their father.

Sometimes I think my relationship with them has been a rerun of my relationship with my father—especially when it comes to Joey. Believe me, I did everything I could to dump that movie! But it's not so easy. You can't just say, Okay now I'll behave in such and such a way. It doesn't work like that—at least not for me. The only thing I can hope is that I restrained myself often enough so my actions were at least a watered-down version of my father and me.

Anyway, maybe they have done some things that didn't make me happy, but I was no prize for much of my life. It was always about me and what I wanted. Not that I would intentionally hurt someone. That doesn't make me a bad person, does it? I wonder what my mother and father would have to say about that.

There were so many special moments that I shared with the kids and so many things they did that made me proud. Too many to mention here. Well, to be honest, I can't remember them all now. But believe me, there were many.

I have to put all this down in writing and give the letters to Monique so she can pass them on to the kids after I'm gone.

MONIQUE
SAUL'S WILL

Today was a disaster. Several weeks back, Saul had suggested that we go downtown to see Nat Friedman, our family lawyer for the last thirty years. Actually, Saul's lawyer and boyhood friend. I told Saul last night that we had to be in Nat's office this morning at ten thirty. He had a puzzled look on his face. So I reminded him that it had been his idea to meet with Nat as soon as he returned from some legal conference over in Hong Kong. Saul has been going downhill and said he wanted to put his affairs in order while he was still well enough.

Saul became agitated. "How dare you try to interfere," he said. No, make that shouted—shouted so loud, in fact, that they could probably hear him all the way down on Sherbrooke Street. He said all I wanted was his money. That I didn't give a rat's ass—what a disgusting expression—about him. I sat through his tirade, which lasted only a few moments but seemed to go on forever. When he was finished, he got up and went into the kitchen, looking, I was sure, for the bottle of scotch that I had hidden under the counter. Dr. Tremblay told me it was okay for him to have a glass or two, but not his usual three or four.

I waited for him to storm back into the living room, accusing me of hiding it. But there was only silence. A few moments later, I went into the kitchen. He was sitting at the table, staring at the napkin holder. I figured it wouldn't do any good to bring up the subject of our meeting again, so I helped him up from his chair and guided him into the bedroom beside the den.

I had moved our bedroom down from the second floor a couple of weeks before, knowing that as Saul got worse, the stairs would become not only an annoyance but dangerous.

This morning, I woke him up at seven thirty and went into the kitchen to make breakfast while he got into the clothes that I'd laid out for him. It breaks my heart to watch him stare at a sock or a shoe, trying to figure out what to do with it. Sometimes it's no problem, and other times I have to come back in the room and rearrange him. Today, he did it right and came into the kitchen with a smile on his face.

"We're going to see Nat this morning," he said, as if we had never discussed it.

I nodded as I placed his favorite pecan-and-banana pancakes with Quebec maple syrup in front of him. Although I sometimes wonder why I don't just use the cheaper fake syrup, because, at this point, I don't think he can tell the difference. But I would feel like a traitor if I did that.

He always made such a big deal of knowing if it was the real stuff. He would sometimes put his hands over his eyes and dare me to trick him. "Go ahead, *chou-fleur*, try to fool me," he would say. That was his favorite name for me. It sounds better in French than cauliflower, its English translation. But he doesn't say it in either language anymore.

Nat couldn't have been nicer. He listened patiently as Saul rambled on about how he had scored a hole in one on the par three, seventh hole at the golf club we used to belong to. Not only was that fifteen years ago, but Nat was playing in the same foursome.

After about ten minutes, Nat changed the conversation to a power of attorney for when Saul wouldn't be able to handle his own affairs. I sat there, squirming in my seat. I knew that even though Saul and maybe others wouldn't think me capable of counting past ten on my fingers, I was the one who should handle everything. Who else would have Saul's best interest at heart? And who else loves the children as much as I do and would look out for them? And I'm no imbecile. You don't have to go to school and get a degree to have common sense.

Nat asked me if I would share with him the duties of administering the power of attorney, or living mandate, as he called it, when Saul could no longer cope, as well as be an executor of Saul's will. I looked over at Saul. He was fumbling with the tassel on his loafer. I wanted him to say something, to give me permission. Finally, Nat asked him what he thought. He looked over at me and mumbled, "There's no way."

Nat could see me turning red. He got up and whispered something in Saul's ear. Then he put on his kindest face and asked me if I would mind waiting in the conference room across the hall for just a few minutes. I started to shake, but I stood up, pushed back my shoulders, and left the office.

It was as if Saul had stabbed me with the big knife in the top drawer by the stove. Why do I stay with this man? A man who doesn't trust me. A man who feels he has to control me.

I gave up everything for him—my religion, my identity, and, yes, even my freedom. I wanted to go back to school to get a college degree. Saul would have none of it. He said it wasn't worth it. Frankly, I think he didn't want me to be out of the house for too long. He always complained that I didn't have a job, but if I tried, and I did, no matter how small it was without a degree, he would somehow find a way to stop me. And if he couldn't, he would belittle me. And I, like an idiot, would let him do so. Sometimes I think God is punishing me for leaving the Church. Not that I had been a zealot, but I did attend Mass every Sunday and went to confession when necessary, or should I say, when I was racked with guilt.

Regardless, I belonged to something. Now what do I belong to? We're not members of any clubs or any community organizations anymore. And except for the High Holidays, we don't attend services at the synagogue. And when we do go, I look around and feel so out of place, like I'm not one of them. And I guess I'm not.

The bottom line is, I belong to Saul, like a piece of chattel. I have always felt I had to be on call for his every whim and desire and that I couldn't have a normal social life with any of my old friends.

Saul doesn't like it if I speak French. I think it's because his French is limited, and when I am with other French people in a social situation with him, he isn't in control. He's basically alienated my old friends by making what I believe were intentional comments that could be perceived as bigoted—borderline things, but whatever they were, they were offensive enough so that most of them don't call anymore.

You may be thinking to yourself, If she wanted to have a life, why didn't she just go out and do it? It wasn't that easy. He was domineering and overbearing and could make me feel so small—so wrong, even when I knew I was right. Nothing I did ever seemed to please him. Now, though, he needs me. So what am I going to do? Leave him? No, I've made my lot in life. And for better or worse, I'm Saul's wife.

They were in there for thirty-four minutes—I timed it. Nat knocked on the door and came into the conference room alone. His face was cheerless as he told me in a halting voice that in his opinion Saul was too far gone to execute either a living mandate or a will. So the will and living mandate that he had modified five years ago would remain valid. I never knew he'd changed them five years ago, so I wondered if that was a good thing or a bad thing.

SAUL

MY WILL

She's pushing me around like some kind of kid in the playground.
I mean, I'm still okay, not gone off the deep end—yet. Why can't
she just let me be? Let me have the last whatever time I have to be
happy. But that's not her style. She's still as pushy as ever, still the
master controller. Still wants to run the damn show.

Today was a perfect example. She must have called Nat
Friedman sometime during the night. I heard some noises while
I was tossing and turning in bed. At first, I thought it was the cat,
but I don't think we have one. And besides, the sounds were too
big. So it must have been her in cahoots with Friedman. I've suspected them for a long time. They're trying to steal my money, making sure my final days are miserable and denying the kids what is
rightfully theirs. Friedman was always a money-grubber. One of
those two-bit lawyers who prey on their clients by jacking up fees
to whatever they think they can get away with. He's done it to me,
to Arthur Winslow, to everyone who goes to him. Why we keep
going back, I don't know, except they're all the same. I remember
Jeff Miller, a big-shot tax lawyer with one of the major firms in the
city. I referred a friend to him, and he hosed him so badly for doing

almost nothing. Worse thing was, he didn't even do what little work there was. He passed it down to some minion, showed up for a couple of meetings, and then sent a bill that would have sunk the *Titanic*—but that's another story.

I can accept the overcharging, but I don't think someone like Friedman should use his fancy degree and being a member of the Quebec Bar—big deal, member of the Bar—to take advantage of Monique. Although my guess is that the last few years she didn't need a lot of coaxing. I think she's been fooling around for a long time. But Friedman, he's supposed to be my friend. Some friend, speaking to my wife in the middle of the night, conspiring to get rid of me so they can be together and steal all my money.

Well, I showed them today. Friedman wanted to be the guy who handles my stuff while I'm alive and wanted Monique to help him. Do I look like a schmuck? I know they're both like vultures waiting for their prey to die so they can suck on its sweet flesh. They want the right to kill me. Yes, that's correct—kill me. When you sign one of those things, and if you're a little bit off your rocker, or in a . . . you know, like a deep-sleep thing, they can tell the doctor to kill you. In two seconds, they can send you to heaven or hell.

So I sat there and listened and nodded and whatever, and they thought I was being suckered by their sneaky plan. But when Monique left the room, I told Friedman I wasn't going to let them do me in. He gave me one of his phony endearing smiles and assured me that wasn't the case.

"What is the case?" I asked.

He said he was only trying to help me, to look after me, to watch over the family, Joey, Bernie, Florence, and, of course, Monique.

"Yeah, I bet you're going to look out for the family," I said. I told him I knew about him and Monique.

Again he plastered that sympathetic smile of his on his face, like he was so sorry for my inability to see the truth. Sometimes I think they take a full semester in law school learning how to do that smile. Friedman must have got an A. Anyway, I told him he wasn't going to be the one who decided anything about my money, or when I die. He put his hand on my arm and asked me to reconsider, again giving me that damn beaming grin of his. God, I would have liked to have dented a few of those too-white teeth of his. But then he probably has big connections with the police, being a big-shot lawyer and all. And I didn't want to spend my last days in some stinking jail having those perverts try to make me their girl, or whatever you call it. Those guys are sick, really sick. Sicker than me. Can you imagine big macho guys doing that stuff to each other? No wonder they send them to jail!

Enough of that. Let me tell you how I handled the will thing. You see, at first, before I knew that Monique was fooling around, I was leaving her everything, so long as she took care of the kids and willed them whatever was left when she was gone. So while she was sitting in Friedman's conference room, filing her nails, or whatever women do when they have nothing to do—which in Monique's case is often. I mean volunteer work at the YMCA . . . big deal. She never really worked. I mean never had a real job. She always said she wanted to but that she couldn't find work because she had no experience. Then when she got older, she said no one wanted to hire a woman her age. Gimme a break. If she wanted to get off her fat tush and find a job, she could have. But she preferred to have me sweat day and night to make the money while she played mahjong with her fancy lady friends. Well, they say you always marry your mother!

Anyway, while she was in there, I discussed it all with Friedman. Yeah, I decided to keep Friedman as my lawyer. I'm getting too sick to start changing at this point, and they're all crooks anyway. He told me maybe I should just keep everything as is and that if I want to make changes in the future, I should let him know. That makes sense, I guess, because first of all, I'll be damned if I'll pay him to change my will twice—there would be almost nothing left! And besides, I'll see how Monique behaves. Maybe I'll leave her something; maybe I won't.

SAUL
FIRST CONFESSION

I heard Monique talking to Florence on the phone. At least I think it was Florence, because she called her "honey," like she does sometimes. She never calls Joey that. In fact, when she refers to Joey in conversations with me, she always says "that son of yours," stuff like that.

Now, I know Joey is her son. I was at the hospital when she gave birth, although it was hard to watch. I'm just like Florence; I can't stand the sight of blood. When Joey came out covered with the stuff, my whole body shook, like when my father would roll his tongue between his teeth and hit me when I was a kid. He did that a lot, and I was always waiting for his tongue to drop to the ground and blood to pour from his mouth. But that never happened.

It seemed he was always hitting or kicking me under the dining room table, and that hurt, because I never thought I had done anything wrong. I already told you I was a tough guy, but I was a fair tough guy.

Joey and Monique were born under different signs. He is a Taurus, and she is an Aquarius. But I'm an Aquarius, too, and I love Joey. I'm not saying she doesn't have any feelings for him, but they're not the same as her feelings for Florence. Sure, he isn't as easy as Florence, but so what. I probably wasn't as easy as my sister, Miriam, but my father should have loved me, too.

Monique asked Florence to go shopping for things to child-proof our house. No one told me that I was going to be a grandfather again. That's wonderful news!

She's been gone a long time. Maybe she is seeing someone else. She has been acting a bit funny lately. My guess is that she wants to leave me and doesn't know how to tell me because I'm sick. Well, I wish she would just do it and get it over with.

I have always been faithful to Monique—except for one affair with Gisele at the paper company. I already was the owner by that time, and she was my secretary. She didn't have knockers like Monique, but she had legs like that actress—what's her name . . . yeah, Marilyn Monroe—and she showed them off, especially when she bent over the file cabinet. She was young, real young. I don't mean young enough for me to get in trouble with the police.

I would always close up the office. She generally stayed late, and one night things just happened. I never felt particularly guilty about it because I didn't love Gisele, but she did do things to me Monique never had.

I asked Monique one day, after Gisele showed me some of her tricks, if she would, well, you know . . .

Monique told me I was a disgusting pig, or words to that effect. My father was right: you don't marry Jewish women for sex. I guess that includes converted Catholics. Not that we didn't have sex, but let's just say they should have named the missionary position the rabbi position.

MONIQUE
THE ULTIMATE CONSUMER

Typically, I don't leave Saul alone in a room for more than a few minutes at a time, and that's usually when I'm doing my housework or calling the store to deliver groceries.

Now I have come to realize that a lot can happen in just a few minutes. It started with subscriptions to *Time* magazine and *Newsweek*. And then there was the aluminum siding. It seems that a telemarketer had called and convinced Saul that new siding would enhance the appearance of the house. When the installation man called to make an appointment, I had to inform him that since the house was brick, it wouldn't be a good idea to put aluminum siding over it. He laughed, thinking I was joking, but when I insisted, he said he had a contract guaranteed by a credit card and would have someone from accounting call me to straighten things out.

But the best was yet to come. Last Tuesday afternoon, the doorbell rang. I looked through the front window and saw a Fournier Carpets truck. When I opened the door, two men stood there with a work order to clean the wall-to-wall carpet in the living room. That would have been fine, except we have oak floors and antique Oriental rugs.

I talked my way out of all of those, and the people were very nice. One who wasn't so nice was the life insurance salesman who arrived at seven o'clock two weeks ago, having made an appointment with Saul. I explained that my husband has Alzheimer's and that we wouldn't be needing his help. He said that was even more reason I should buy a policy on my life, since he obviously figured out he couldn't sell one on what was left of Saul's days on this earth. When I apologized for the third time and started to close the door, he stuck his foot between the door and the frame long enough to give me a piece of his mind. Saul heard the commotion and came out from the living room. Even after I had explained Saul's situation, the man started in on him. What kind of horrible person would do that?

I slammed the door, and the man's foot in the process. It took only three days to receive a letter from his lawyer. That's another thing I'll have to deal with, on top of everything else.

SAUL

A SOLID LEFT HOOK

When I went into the kitchen, Monique's mascara was running, as usual. Her head was tucked into her knockers and her whole body was heaving. I asked her what had happened.

She looked up and pointed her finger at me. "Don't you ever do that again," she shouted, "or I'll have you put away!"

"Do what?" I asked. It wasn't her mascara running—I mean, yes, it was running, but she had an ugly bruise under her right eye. I asked her what had happened, and she glared at me. She has learned over the years to copy my Reimer stare. I say copy, because It doesn't have the same intensity as mine, but it's a pretty good imitation, nonetheless.

She claimed that I'd slugged her. Now one thing I would never do is hit a woman. Not that some of them didn't deserve it at times, including Monique and that holier-than-thou mother of mine. My mother would never punish me; she would just advise me that Larry would take care of all that stuff when he got home from work. She was like the announcer on television who would tell the viewers that so-and-so would be on next—so stay tuned! And the first thing she would say to my father when he walked through the door was, "Do you know what your son did today?"

That was all Larry needed. Frankly, he didn't need her help. He could have found something I did wrong all by himself, and generally did, even before his first scotch, at least the first scotch he drank at home. My father always reeked of liquor when he arrived home from work. His biggest accounting client must have been Johnnie Walker!

Anyway, regardless of whether or not a woman deserves a beating, Saul Reimer is not the one to administer it. So, no, I didn't hit Monique. I may be getting . . . no, I know I am getting worse, but that isn't something I would ever do, no matter how bad I get.

"So who did it?" I asked her. Was she fooling around, and her lover belted her because she wouldn't do those tricks he liked? When I said that, she pushed me aside and ran into her bedroom, sobbing. I say her bedroom, because even though we share a bed in there, everything else is hers, and everything is pink or yellow.

She slammed the door so hard, it made my head hurt. My head seems to hurt quite a bit lately. I can't stand the noise of the vacuum cleaner or the washing machine. Monique says the house has to function and that I need fresh clothes. When I have an accident, I throw my underwear into the trash by the back door. Somehow it reappears in my drawer, clean and neatly folded, but we never talk about it.

SAUL
CORROBORATION OF MY DEATH SENTENCE

Monique isn't angry with me today. In fact, she took me for sushi in the basement of Westmount Square, a tall, boxy group of three black buildings—or maybe four. She pulled out my chair. I hate it when she does that, so I pushed it back in and accidentally knocked over the soy sauce thing. She scooped it off the table and put it on an empty table beside us. We both stood there—she with her hands on her hips, looking at me; me staring through her.

We finally sat down, but not before I pulled her chair out. She smiled and then asked me if I wanted soup or salad to start.

I said, "Soup or salad."

She asked, "Which one, soup or salad?"

I replied, "Damn it, I said soup."

She said, "Maybe you should have the salad; you may spill the soup."

A young Oriental girl brought the salad. I winked at her and held out my hand. She seemed a bit startled.

Monique grabbed my arm and yanked it away, apologizing to her at the same time. Something about my having the big A disease. The girl offered a faint smile and left the ordering and writing things in front of us. Monique said she would do it for us. I told her I could do it for myself and was going to order for her, too.

She touched my arm, and I shrugged her off. I picked up the writing thing and asked her what she wanted. She told me. I searched the menu for a long time but couldn't find it.

"They don't have it," I finally said. "Pick something else."

She said, "They have it; I'll check it off."

She picked up her writing thing and made a quick check. I scrunched my eyes together, opened them wide, and put my own checks on the menu. Then I waved it in front of me to get the young girl's attention. She reached over the table from Monique's side and plucked it out of my hand.

In what seemed like just moments later, she put two plates in front of me.

"I didn't order this," I said.

She wanted to know what I'd ordered.

"I don't remember," I said, my eyes tearing, "but not this."

She looked at Monique and nodded.

Monique said, "Why don't you eat it anyway, dear; it looks delicious?"

I replied, "I will not," and pushed back my chair and folded my arms across my chest.

Monique asked for the bill. Then, while we waited, she told me she'd gotten me something, and pulled a small box out of her purse. It was a silver bracelet. The front said MedicAlert. The back had a toll-free 800 number, the words *Memory Impaired—Allergic to Penicillin—Call Immediately*, and my new moniker, 344689. She slung it over my wrist and locked it into place, branding me like they do cattle. That made it official. Saul Reimer, number 344689, has Alzheimer's.

FLORENCE
HE'S STILL A HUMAN BEING

Mother and I have just come back from seeing Dr. Tremblay to discuss Father's results. Dr. Tremblay said he was already into the middle stage, which he told us is normal, considering it's been three years since he was diagnosed. That was no surprise. But nonetheless, the way he has been acting lately has frightened me. What were occasional behaviors are now normal. And what was the norm is now only occasional.

I look at him the same way. But I notice that Joey, and to some extent Mother, treat him like the disease that has taken over his existence. He may have lost a lot and be unable to function like we do, but he isn't a vegetable and shouldn't be treated like one.

The other day, he wanted to wear his favorite paisley tie, one that Mother has always felt was gaudy. Now that Father is basically powerless to resist, Mother told him he couldn't wear it. I mean, what's the big deal? She said he wouldn't know the difference, and she wanted him to look good when she took him for lunch at Westmount Square. But I could see the sparkle leave his eyes as she reached over his broad shoulders to tie a knot on the boring brown tie.

What about his pride and self-esteem? He still has that left, but he won't for long if they continue to paint him as if he's already gone, as some sort of contaminated subhuman being. I believe, and I have told them both, that we should do whatever we think he wants, not what we want, so that the remaining time he has living at home can be as comfortable as possible for him. Dr. Tremblay said there is no use in correcting him when he makes a mistake. All that will do is upset him, and he won't remember anyway.

Now, more than ever, he needs to feel our love and caring— even if Joey has to fake it. He was good at faking it when he needed money from Father, so it really shouldn't be too difficult for him. I think Mother, although they have quarreled since I can remember, really does love Father, or at least cares for him. So even if it means biting her tongue and letting him do what he wants, why shouldn't she?

He may not be able to function normally, but he isn't just Saul Reimer, a middle-stage Alzheimer's victim, whose worth is the sum total of the results of all the tests he has taken. He is my father, a man, and a human being.

SAUL

QUICKSAND

Last night, I had a dream.

I am walking down an endless highway. One of those two-lane roads that goes on forever. The pavement changes to some kind of Jell-O, but I continue walking through it as if it were still the real road. Suddenly, the Jell-O starts to attack me. I try to move my feet. They're stuck. I start to sink in slow motion, until the gooey liquid is up to my neck.

My parents, Hannah and Larry, appear in front of me. They look like that painting of the farmer with the pitchfork and his wife. My father says it's almost over. My mother looks sad. Then my sister, Miriam, appears. I reach out to take her hand, but before I can grab it, they all vanish, and in their place stand Monique, Florence, and Joey. They hold out their hands. I reach out once more. This time, Monique takes my hand and pulls me out. I look down and can see my feet on the pavement. The three of them disappear, and I start to walk down the road again. Moments later, the Jell-O attacks me and I start to sink. Then I woke up.

MONIQUE
THE VASE

I went into the kitchen this morning, drained from spending more than two hours following Saul around the house. Last night's escapade started in our bedroom and took a circuitous route up and down the stairs and, more than once, through every room except for the garage.

I walked into the dining room, as I usually do with my morning coffee, and sat at the long mahogany table with its cushioned Regency-style chairs. A lone crystal vase sat in the middle, filled with white roses. I usually change them every ten days or so, but I didn't have a chance to get new ones this week, what with Saul being more difficult and demanding than usual. I'm not complaining. Well, maybe I am. But having a few minutes to brood and feel sorry for myself is not a crime. Wouldn't you agree?

I glanced over at the white petals that had fallen onto the table. Most days, there are usually only a few. But today there were more petals on the table than on the wilted roses. And they were strewn about, probably as a result of a breeze from the open window.

I've sat here almost every morning for years, staring at the roses. After finishing my coffee, I would pick up the petals that had fallen to the table and put them in the trash. But today, for the first time, I realized the obvious. That as each petal falls, a flower loses a part of its life. And that's what's happening to Saul. Bit by bit, he is losing parts of himself, and eventually, when all the petals fall, he will be nothing—gone—extinct. My poor Saul.

SAUL
I AM DYING

Not a quick death, unfortunately, but a gradual shutting down of my system that will probably get me to hell and back many times before the Lord takes me. I have thought about cheating him and taking the easy way out. In fact, I bought a book called *Final Exit*, about taking your life, after Dr. Horowitz first told me I might have Alzheimer's. I hid it underneath some old tax statements in the den. I had forgotten exactly where I'd put it, but I came across it while I was tidying up today. For some reason, it comes tightly wrapped in plastic. I unwrapped it but only got as far as reading the back cover. It says right there on the back that it offers people with a terminal illness a choice on how and when to end their suffering.

Here's the conundrum. Amazing! A fifty-cent word that I not only remembered but, I think, used in the right place. I may be going crazy, but I am not going stupid! Anyway, the doctors have told me, and I don't mean one or two, but more, including Dr. Tremblay and some neuro guy and a couple of others. They have told me I probably have Alzheimer's, but they say they can't be 100 percent sure until after I die and they open my head to see if I have that plaque stuff on my brain. They're pretty sure, more than pretty sure, but not 100 percent sure.

My best guess is that I am heading pretty fast toward my demise. I plan to start reading the book before it just looks like a bunch of jumbled letters with no meaning. In fact, I already seem to mix up some of the letters in words, so I'd better do it soon.

The doctors have me on so many pills, I can hardly see the kitchen counter. Ginkgo, Aricept, and something called Melamine or Memantine or something. You would think I would know the right name, given I take so many of them. They're all supposed to slow down my memory loss, or at least the symptoms. So far, they tell me it seems to be working like it should, but then again, how would I know what is normal? There is nothing normal in this hell I'm in.

Yesterday, we went to Dr. Tremblay's office. He wanted me to be part of a test group, one where they give some of us the real thing and the others what he called a . . . well, anyway, it was the fake one.

Monique said she wanted the doctor to give me the real thing. The doctor said he couldn't guarantee it, but that I had a 50 percent chance. The drug was like an experiment or something, and the only way I could possibly get it was to be part of the group. Monique went ballistic. I have never seen her so angry. She told the doctor in a loud voice that I was a human being, not a guinea pig. Sometimes I think Monique loves me.

MONIQUE
HOW SAD FOR HIM, HOW SAD FOR ME

Saul was sitting in front of the television, a blank look on his face. He seemed so sad, so empty. And he has every right to be that way. What does he have to look forward to? What quality of life? What happiness? It takes him forever to get dressed. His taste buds are diminishing. The doctor said he's all but lost his sense of smell. *Mon Dieu*, that's half the enjoyment of eating. And I always seem to be cutting up his food when we go out. I know he can sort of do it most of the time, but I am tired of being embarrassed in public. Mind you, having people watch me cut his meat isn't exactly a pleasure, either.

He certainly can't enjoy wearing clothes like he used to. He doesn't seem to be able to focus on a book anymore, and his patience when it comes to playing cards or games is almost nonexistent. As far as I'm concerned, he has no quality of life. And he is really getting depressed. I do everything I can to distract him from all the desolation he must be going through, but it's a losing battle.

Maybe he'd be better off dead, and maybe I'd be better off, too.

I know you are probably saying to yourself, What a shrew she is! Her poor husband is ill, dying a slow, wretched death, and she's there pitying herself. That may be how it appears, but it's not the case. I wish people could understand what I go through every day. They all feel sorry for Saul. What about me?

I feel like I'm almost invisible. People hardly ever ask how I'm doing, and when they do, it's seems like they are asking because they feel they have to, but they really couldn't care less. No one gives me any support. I'm not going to go to one of those caretaker support groups. First of all, I can't see how a bunch of people stuck in the same boat are going to be able to help one another. And I'm not going to have some social worker lecture me. Besides, as I've told you before, I can't leave Saul alone.

Florence does come by, and Joey breezes in and out, usually for ten minutes. And Saul has a couple of friends, like Arthur Winslow, who visit on a regular basis. But I am the one stuck alone here every day, wandering the house with him at night, being the object of his physical abuse, carrying wet naps in my purse to wipe his drool. My God, what's next?

Do you know that I'm on Valium to control my anxiety? That my stomach is on fire all day, and that I'm practically addicted to Tagamet? That I now carry nitroglycerin in my purse for my heart condition?

I wish I could just tell someone all that—someone who cares and would understand. I've tried with Florence, but although she listens and offers some comfort, I know it's her father she's concerned about. And forget Joey, that would be a waste of time. Dr. Tremblay said I should feel free to call him if I were experiencing any difficulty, but when I called him, he just said he would send over a refill for my Valium prescription. Saul may be the one with Alzheimer's, but I'm the one suffering a long and miserable life.

SAUL

I'M NOT GONE YET

I know it's sunset for me, but that's not the worst part. The worst part is what's her name, yeah, Monique. She seems to think I'm all but a goner with a miserable life. Actually, when she's not around to bully me, I'm fairly content. Well, *content* may not be the right word, but it's close enough. I mean, I kind of enjoy watching television, even if I miss a lot of what's going on. It's a miracle if I can concentrate until the end of a program. Although, for the most part, I can in the morning, but it gets almost impossible as the day goes on, especially with those damn commercials. Sometimes I feel like they stick them in there just to see if I can remember what was going on in the show— sort of a test to see how far gone I am. But I'm still here, although maybe not driving in the fast lane.

I still sort of enjoy my food, but one look at my belly would tell you that. I would really like it if we ate at some of my favorite restaurants, but Monique rarely takes me out anymore. My best guess is that she hates cutting my food in front of people. I would really like it if I could do it myself, but it would take hours, and probably most of the meal would end up on the floor. Unfortunately, there's nothing I can do about that.

She's always asking me if I'm depressed. I didn't think I was, but when she keeps insinuating—wow, another big word—that I am, I figure she must be right.

It's like when my father used to tell me what a nothing I was. I didn't want to make a liar of him, so that's what I became—a nothing—at least till I moved out of his house. But when I move out of this house, I really will be a nothing!

So, am I depressed? Yes, I'm depressed. Who wouldn't be? But I'll be frank with you. The reason I'm depressed is not because of the disease, but because of her. I know what the disease is, what it means, and how it will end. But I am not there yet, and she just doesn't get that.

MONIQUE
NOW WHAT?

When I came into the kitchen this afternoon, the kettle was in the refrigerator and a bunch of rags sat in the bottom of the dishwasher. I looked out the open window. Saul was in the garden, walking around the flower bed. I could hear him mumbling to himself, "I have to get home, I have to get home."

I went outside and asked him what he was doing. He didn't look up and didn't stop pacing. So I put myself in front of him. He pushed me aside and kept going.

I said, "Saul, you are home."

He looked over his shoulder and asked who I was. I told him I was his wife, Monique. He laughed.

A few minutes later, Florence stopped by on her way back from the office. Frankly, I don't know why she still works. She and Bernie don't need the money, given that his clothing business has done so well. She's going to end up a bigger wreck than I am, what with the work, the kids, Bernie, and now her father. I worry about her.

Saul was pacing even faster now. Florence wanted to go outside and stop him. I said, "What for? Maybe he'll get tired and sleep a little tonight." He dozes off a lot during the day and keeps waking up at night. And sometimes he'll get out of bed and just wander around the house. I can't let him go by himself, so I follow him. Last night, he was up for over an hour, searching for his father. I tried to explain that his father was dead, but that didn't go over too well. He screamed, "I'm going to find him, and when I do, I'm going to give him a licking!"

I know the doctor said not to argue with him or correct him, because he probably won't remember what I say anyway. But sometimes I get so frustrated that I want to tear my hair out.

I made a pot of coffee, took some macaroons out of the ceramic jar in the pantry, and put them on the table. Florence kept staring out the window. I could see the tears welling up in her tired eyes. I used to watch him, too, but now I figure there's nowhere he can go, so why drive myself crazy?

I told Florence about an incident last week with her father. He was screaming at the top of his lungs from the basement that there was an intruder in the house and I should call the police. I wasn't sure what to do. I grabbed a kitchen knife and tiptoed over to the back stairs. All I could hear was him still yelling for me to call for help. I slowly made my way down the stairs. Saul was standing by the pool table, pointing. "There he is, there he is," he kept saying.

"I don't see anyone, *mon cher*," I said, my hand still gripping the knife tightly in my fist.

He gestured toward the mirror in front of him. "Why don't you call them?" he begged, "before he attacks us."

I took his arm, turned him around, and led him back upstairs.

SAUL

MY MOTHER

"I can't find it," I screamed for the zillionth time. "Damn it! I can't find it!"

Monique rushed into the room and asked me what I was looking for. My forehead scrunched up, and I slammed my fist into the wall.

"What?" she asked again. This time, her voice was only a whisper in the distance.

The wall suddenly took on different shades of yellow and orange, dancing in front of me like a well-orchestrated symphony. The notes zoomed in and out, faster and faster. Then, just as swiftly as they appeared, they vanished. Now the wall was once again its same old bland color. My head felt like a truck had rolled over it and reversed for good measure.

"What were you looking for, *mon cher?*" Monique asked softly, as she drew me to her bosom.

"I don't know," I replied. And I didn't. I had a vague recollection that I had been searching for something, but it was only a distant thought. This wasn't the first time I had blanked, and according to Dr. Tremblay, it wouldn't be the last.

It's ironic that I had often blanked—even when God wasn't yet robbing me of my memory—when I was trying to reconstruct some of my childhood recollections.

Sure, I remembered splashing in the ocean off Cape Cod. Going to the lobster pound and staring into the dark blue tank that housed what seemed like thousands of giant lobsters, which were fighting and clawing to get nowhere but to my paper plate, alongside the fries and creamy coleslaw. And, of course, there was the merry-go-round at the amusement park, and the ever-present cotton candy on my chin. But those were the times spent with my aunt and uncle and cousins from Ontario.

My father was usually too busy to go with us, and my mother was often a no-show, depending on her social schedule, or perhaps I should say her "socialite" schedule. My mother's calling on this earth was not to see, but to be seen. She loved being seen by the photographers from the Montreal *Gazette*, especially the ones from the social page, and mingling with the fancy folks who lived off the rarefied oxygen that was pumped only into upper Westmount. And not only was she was good at it; she was the best.

No one could ingratiate herself like Hannah. She was like a salamander, slithering up the hill from our apartment in Snowdon, which was then the Jewish ghetto. She was one of the few who didn't need a special visa to get in, either. Her wardrobe spoke rich, her vocabulary spoke rich, and, to her credit, her sense of style spoke rich. But we weren't rich. Like I told you before, my father was an accountant, but not to the rich. In fact, he hated the rich. Probably because he wasn't and never would be. But my mother dragged him along on most of her outings, his body draped in the same tuxedo that she had bought him for one of his birthdays, instead of the fishing rod he asked for.

My mother was so good at what she did that she once had a woman over for tea who was the wife of one of the wealthiest men in the country. They lived in a mansion up on the hill. Mother all but redecorated the living room for the event. It looked like a movie set. I, of course, was instructed to disappear. But my sister, after much primping and a visit to the hairdresser at the tender age of twelve, was ordered to join the command performance, albeit for five minutes and no more, at which point she was expected to curtsy her way back to reality.

Sometimes I think Mother would have been happier in one of those loveless marriages where everyone gets what they want. She was certainly pretty enough to be a model. And I'm sure there were rich men, even if they were ugly, or old, or both, who would have liked a trophy wife. She probably wouldn't have had to have sex that often. My guess is that she didn't do too much of that with my father anyway, so at least she would have had the status that she so desperately wanted. My sister and I would not have been born, of course, which might not have been good for my sister. But then, she died too early—much too early.

FLORENCE
BERNIE'S VISIT

It seems a lifetime ago that I first met Bernie. He certainly was more boisterous back then, but he's mellowed over the years. Even then, he was kind and compassionate deep down, although it was almost as if he didn't want anyone to know it.

He went over to see Father today without me or the kids. Just the two of them. That took a lot of guts, given how Father feels about him. What no one knows, except Father, Bernie, and me—not even Mother—is that I became pregnant while we were in college. We found out two weeks after our engagement. The wedding was to be the following year, after graduation. A big affair at the Windsor Hotel. Something Mother insisted on, even though Father could barely afford it.

I told Father, figuring he would be more understanding than Mother. Was I wrong! He was more upset than I have ever seen him. He insisted on my having an abortion. "What would my friends think of a good Jewish girl getting knocked up?" he screamed. "What would they think of your little princess having an abortion?" I retorted.

Once he realized I wasn't going to end the pregnancy, he reluctantly helped us concoct a story in which we had decided to move the wedding up because I would be working right after graduation. That was after he had given the hotel a deposit, but before he had to pay the band a third of their fee in advance.

Naturally, he didn't blame me—I was the innocent victim. Bernie, however, became persona non grata. And it has remained like that to this day. Bernie learned to live with it and still went out of his way to be kind to Father. But believe me, there was no reciprocation. The sad irony of it all is that I had a miscarriage two months later, and it took me almost ten more years to get pregnant with our first son, Howard.

So today, with Father slipping, but still having some semblance of comprehension, Bernie decided to sit down with him and try to make peace.

The way Bernie tells it, the visit didn't start off very well, even though he went over in the morning, when Father is generally more lucid. Father accused him of raping me, being a pimp, and other niceties, which even though I'm no prude, I can't repeat here. Bernie said he waited him out, letting him vent.

When Father finished, he slouched back in his chair. Bernie started to speak, but Father raised his hand to stop him. Then he stood up and went over to Bernie, motioning for him to get up. He put his arms out and hugged Bernie and said he was glad he had come, that Bernie was a good father and a good husband, and how sorry he was for his attitude all these years. Then Father returned to his seat, propped his feet up on the ottoman, and asked Bernie how the kids were. And that was it. A few seconds later, he got up and turned on the television, as if Bernie wasn't in the room. But Bernie said he didn't care, that it was one of the best days of his life.

SAUL
MY LAST PLACE ON EARTH

It's all unraveling.

Last night, I found myself somewhere on Monkland Avenue. I had no idea how I got there. I looked in a store window and saw my reflection. It took me a bit to figure it all out—like that the person in the window was a man, and that the man was me.

I didn't know what to do. I glanced down at the bracelet on my wrist and everything—well, not everything, but the gist of it all came back to me. I am Saul Reimer, formerly a healthy, intelligent man, married to the same woman for many years, and the father of two children he loves more than anything in the world.

The key word is *formerly*, as I am sure you've already figured out. Because today—and I have no idea what day it is, other than it is really cold and I wish I had a jacket on—I am nothing, not a real man, that's for sure. I mean, how can you be a real man when you don't even know where you are half the time, and when you do know, more often than not, you can't grasp the concept of your surroundings?

I felt in my pocket for my wallet, but it wasn't there. All I had was my bank card. I spotted an ATM machine at the corner. But when I got there, I couldn't figure out how to work it. A woman walked up from behind. I gestured for her to go in front of me. She smiled and said she was in no rush. I looked at the machine, with all the words flashing across the screen. My hands were getting slimy, and beads of that wet stuff covered my forehead. Why couldn't she just go first?

Then suddenly, it all made sense. I followed the directions, but it took me a few tries to get the card into the machine with the strip the right way. I looked behind me again. The woman was fidgeting with her purse strap. Then the machine asked me for a personal identification number. The good news is, I knew I had one. The bad news is, I had no idea what it was. My brain is like a shortwave radio, mostly static that occasionally finds the station, but even then the sound isn't always clear.

In a way, it will be a blessing when my mind is totally gone, when I am a vegetable, slouched in a wheelchair. Like many Alzheimer's patients on Montreal's West Side, I'll probably make a pit stop at Manoir Laurier. Then, when Manoir Laurier can't cope with me, or we can't afford it anymore, they'll ship me off to Belfrage Hospital, my final stop on this beloved earth. I'll be there, incontinent, drooling, and incoherent—that is, if I can even manage to get a word through my blistered lips. And when it's all over—when my heart finally gives out, or I contract pneumonia, and my family says, "Let Saul go; he deserves some peace"—when that happens, they'll take me down to the autopsy room, cut my skull open, and find the tangles and plaques on my brain. Then they will be able to say with 100 percent certainty that Saul Reimer had Alzheimer's.

85

MONIQUE
I HAVE TO STAY CALM

Saul slipped out of the house while I was making dinner last night. I guess I didn't hear the chimes on the door because the radio was on. The police told me they'd found him all the way down on Monkland Avenue. They said he looked dazed, and at first they thought he was drunk, but when they saw the bracelet on his wrist, they called the 800 number and brought him home.

And then today—and it's not the first time—I watched him do the same thing over and over and over. Here's what he does: He takes the books off the shelves, one by one, until you can't see the floor. Then he tries to arrange them in some sort of order, but he gives up in disgust and haphazardly shoves them back again. No sooner has he finished than he dumps them on the floor and starts trying to organize them once again. And he babbles like an absent-minded professor while he's doing it.

When he's not rearranging the books, he's in the kitchen, emptying the cupboards and filling them up again. And when he's done with that, he dumps Dugin's dog biscuits into a large plastic bag and carries them into the bedroom, where he hides them beside the dresser. Sometimes I wait a few minutes before retrieving them, but most of the time Dugin is trailing behind him and drags the bag to his cushion by the back door.

By the end of the day, I am so worn-out that I can hardly stand. It used to be I could escape during the week for at least a few hours when I did my volunteer work, but Saul's been too far gone for me to be absent at all.

Dr. Tremblay told me I need my strength in order to be an effective caregiver. He said if I didn't get someone to come to the house, or put Saul in an adult daycare center, I would fall apart and be no good to anyone. Well, there is no way I am going to have someone else take care of him in my house, that's for sure. I mean, even if I wanted to—and I don't—what would people think if I'm out playing mahjong or going to a movie while leaving Saul with hired help?

Last week, we visited the Schaffer Centre. A heavyset woman with stained yellow teeth but a sweet smile nonetheless welcomed us as if we were family. But I knew within minutes that I would never leave Saul there with those blubbering idiots. I don't want you to think that I'm insensitive, but they were like robots—most of them couldn't walk, and they all seemed to be living on another planet.

Saul is heading downhill in slow motion, but a month or two of even a few hours a day there would speed up the process immeasurably. And I'm not going to let that happen.

One of Saul's last joys in life is sitting in that big chair of his in the living room and having Dugin fetch his chewed-up rubber ball. The woman made it very clear there was no chance of him bringing Dugin to the center, even on a leash.

I don't think Saul could exist without that damn dog. It's like they understand each other, even now. Saul laughs, and Dugin barks. Saul cries, and Dugin whimpers. They're inseparable. I think if he had a choice between the dog and me, Dugin would win. And after going through days like today, I sometimes think I wouldn't mind that.

SAUL

MIRIAM

She was really quite pretty and smart. A bit on the skinny side, maybe a bit more than a bit. I like that—"a bit more than a bit." I'll have to remember that one. Fat chance of that!

Anyway, what else can I tell you about Miriam? Let's see—a great musician. She played the flute, clarinet, and saxophone. And she played well, well enough to be first clarinetist of the school orchestra.

But she didn't just have a serious side. She couldn't resist the opportunity to flirt. Even when I would walk home with her, she would bat her long eyelashes at the guys waiting at the bus stop. I think she just wanted to be wanted. I don't think she felt comfortable at home with her overbearing and nutty parents.

Did I tell you about how she would sometimes set up two dates on a Saturday night? I thought only guys did that—you know, one till ten o'clock, then sneaking out and meeting up with the next one at ten thirty. And she was so extraordinary, she got away with it, even if they found out.

When Miriam got older, she looked up to me. But when we were young, it was Miriam who watched out for me. I can't tell you how many times she would bang on my bedroom door, begging my father to stop hitting me. It didn't do any good, but it made me feel better that someone was in my corner. Sometimes I think it hurt her more than me. If that were the case, it must have really hurt her, because I can tell you Larry's belt was made out of the toughest leather ever manufactured!

Miriam graduated from McGill with honors in psychology. With her upbringing, she probably could have passed her exams without even taking the course. I mean, look at all the practical training she had. Hannah and Larry for parents, me for a brother.

Those years at university were wasted. She could have been out having fun, enjoying her life—or whatever she had left of it.

One Saturday afternoon, Miriam called me and asked me to get together with her downtown at Woolworth's. She was going to buy an LP first, and then we'd meet at the snack bar. I hadn't seen her in a while, so we had a lot of catching up to do.

We hung around while she drank her usual coffee with the tons of sugar she liked to dump into her cup, and while I went through two cherry Cokes. Miriam asked me if I wanted to go for a walk on Mount Royal. I was supposed to meet my new girlfriend, Cathy, so I passed. We agreed to get together that night, Cathy and I, Miriam and her new heartthrob—with Miriam there was always one hanging around.

A few blocks later, Miriam was struck by a streetcar. She never made it to the hospital. She was twenty-two. I still miss her.

I can remember the blue skirt and matching wool sweater set she wore that day, and her dark hair combed in a flip. And I can remember her black pumps. Yet today, I can't even remember yesterday.

FLORENCE
SYMPTOMS

The telltale signs are all over the place.

Last Sunday, Father and I were on our way back from the park when he started heading in the wrong direction. I asked him where he was going.

"It doesn't matter," he answered over his shoulder.

I steered him back toward the intersection, but as soon as he saw the redbrick school building, he muttered something about being late for class. He made a beeline for the entrance. I didn't try to stop him, assuming the doors would be locked. But the janitor or someone must have left them open, and he rushed in. Once inside, he raced up the stairs and marched into a classroom.

He stopped in his tracks, eyeing the empty desks neatly lined up in rows that stretched to the back of the room. I couldn't get him to budge from the space he had commandeered. His eyes moved slowly and deliberately, stopping in front of each desk. He mouthed words that were neither intelligible nor of sufficient volume for me to make them out. Then he walked to the back of the room and tried to squeeze his large frame between the seat and the underside of a desk, probably a difficult task in his day, and an impossible one now. Suddenly, he lost his balance and stumbled backward in what seemed like slow motion. When his body finally settled onto the hardwood floor, he opened his eyes and stared up at the ceiling. He held that pose until I reached down and took hold of his arm, guiding him slowly to his feet.

After we left, he began telling me about the good old days at school. He talked animatedly about his different teachers and some of the kids in his classes. It was a normal conversation, like nothing had ever happened.

When we got home, Mother was in the den, waiting. I asked Father to share some of the stories with her. He looked at me like I was crazy and asked me what I was talking about.

Yesterday, I took him to see Dr. Swidler for a checkup. Actually, it was Mother who suggested it. Knowing that it's only a matter of time before he moves into Manoir Laurier, she wanted to make sure he didn't have any problems with his teeth, on top of everything else. The waiting room was full, but there was one empty seat between two Westmount dowagers. I motioned for him to sit between them, but he, ever the gentleman, insisted that I sit down. Normally, I would have argued the point, but frankly, I was afraid of engaging him in any conversation that could lead to his becoming belligerent. So I sat down, and he stood, hovering in front of me.

Celine Dion's voice blasted through the speakers in the ceiling, and the sounds of drilling emanated from behind the door. The women on either side of me were practically spitting in my face as they tried to talk to each other above the Muzak, the drilling, and the nearby conversations.

The cacophony must have gotten to Father. He slammed his hands over his ears and made grunting sounds, his body rocking back and forth. I jumped up, but before I could get my balance, he shoved me back in my seat and rushed through the door to where

Dr. Swidler was working on a patient. I pulled myself up and went after him. By the time I got there, he was standing beside a sink, banging his fist against the wall, shouting, "I can't stand this anymore! I can't stand this anymore!"

MONIQUE
HAPPY BIRTHDAY

Today is Saul's seventy-fifth birthday, a milestone, but not what I was expecting whenever I thought about how we would celebrate—before his illness, that is. It's funny how things happen. I don't count the years numerically anymore; instead, I go by how long it's been since Saul was diagnosed. So this is the end of year four, going on year five.

Florence and Bernie brought the kids, something they hadn't done in a while, not after Saul yelled at Daniel so loudly a few months ago that the poor boy wailed in terror for a good five minutes. It's sad that they will probably remember Saul only the way he is now.

Joey was there, as was Arthur Winslow, Saul's childhood friend. I had baked a carrot cake with the cream cheese icing Saul loves so much. Obviously, I wasn't going to decorate it with seventy-five candles, so I put on three, one for yesterday, one for today, and one for tomorrow.

I had made a collage of Saul's life, including pictures from his childhood that he had kept, pictures of us during our marriage, and both of us with the kids—and with the grandchildren, of course.

Although I must admit he was never much of a grandfather, even before he was sick. It was always an effort even to get him to go to their birthday parties. If I put up a fuss, he usually went, but not with a big smile on his face—until he got there. Then he would take the presents that I'd bought—I always bought one for each of them, so one wouldn't feel left out—and make a big deal about giving them to the grandchildren.

Today, I put up some red and blue streamers between the two lamps by the sofa and a plastic "happy birthday" tablecloth on the dining room table. Because we were only eight people, I didn't bother with a caterer, but I made brisket with sweet potatoes, another of Saul's favorite dishes.

We all sat around in front of the fireplace. The weather was quite mild for February, but I lit a fire anyway. Saul likes to watch it, and it usually keeps him still.

Bernie, Florence, and the children were the first to arrive. Florence bent over to kiss her father and then pushed Daniel and Howard in Saul's direction so they could do the same. I was waiting for the fireworks to start, but Saul bent over so they could reach his cheek, and both of them gave him a quick kiss before retreating. Arthur was the next to arrive, and finally, a half hour later, the king himself, Joey.

Everyone brought a present. I told them not to spend a lot. There wasn't much that Saul could use at this point. Florence brought a bright paisley tie. Why would she do that? I wondered. Arthur brought him a DVD. Joey gave Saul a brush for Dugin. Speaking of Dugin—and I'd rather not, to be honest—he stayed right by Saul's side the whole time.

Bernie took the collage over to the fireplace and put it on the table. We took turns showing Saul the pictures. His eyes sparkled just like in the old days. He put his finger on a photograph of us holding hands in front of the Eiffel Tower, and a big smile came over his face. "Beautiful," he said, "Simply beautiful."

Florence asked him if he knew what birthday it was.

Saul said, "Eight."

"No father," Florence said, "I mean how old are you today?"

Saul closed his eyes for a few seconds but said nothing.

Florence said, "Seventy, seventy-five, eighty, one hundred?"

Saul answered, "The first one."

Florence corrected him. "No, Father, seventy-five. Isn't that great?"

Saul's face tensed and he said again, insistently, "The first one."

I motioned for her to stop before he got agitated, then asked everyone to go to the table. Joey helped Saul out of his easy chair and led him to the seat of honor. We all sat around chatting, mostly about Saul before he got sick. Occasionally, he would jump in, sometimes with appropriate remarks, sometimes with ones completely off base. But, regardless, he was calm and smiling.

After lunch, I lit the candles on the cake, and Joey carried it to the table. I asked Saul to blow them out. He did—two of the three anyway.

Florence put a birthday hat on Saul's head and gave him a party horn. He started to blow the horn, and in between he started laughing, as if he knew something no one else did. It was really quite cute. He was having so much fun, laughing and laughing. After a few minutes, he became quiet, but he stayed seated at the table.

The whole day couldn't have gone better. Everyone left by four. Saul took a nap while I cleaned up. I saved the candles. There won't be many more birthdays.

SAUL

A BIT LEWD

I'm not myself today. Now, that even gives me a tickle. I mean, how can you be yourself when you're morphing into a monster? And by at least one account, I am not only a monster but also a pervert.

Monique told me that today through her running mascara. If she's going to be on a constant crying jag, why doesn't she give up the damn mascara? I mentioned that to her, and all I got was a tongue job. No, I don't mean what you think I mean, but in a way it's all related.

First of all, by tongue job, I mean she kind of stuck her tongue out at me like we did in Miss Novak's grade-three class. You were probably thinking some sex thing, when some of them do the tricks. But like I already told you, Monique doesn't do the tricks.

She said I went into the kitchen last night as naked as God. I guess I'm going to find out if he's wearing clothes soon enough—and frankly, I think I'm ready. Anyway, Monique said I was playing with my thing, and that she told me to stop, but I wouldn't. She said it was repulsive.

I asked her if I'd had an explosion. That really upset her. But I figured it would have been a pity to go through all that and not have an explosion. I can't remember the last time I had one of them with Monique, but given my state, that's probably not news to you. And maybe, just maybe, now that she knows I won't remember much, she tried a couple of those tricks, or at least one of them—you know the one I mean. But I doubt it. I don't think Monique ever had much fun with me when it came to sex. It was always a reward for good behavior. Some reward—a *zaftig* woman with cellulite and stretch marks lying face up on the bed under the bright light, with her eyes squeezed shut, as if awaiting her executioner—not exactly Linda Lovelace in heat!

MONIQUE
HUMILIATION

Saul is really going downhill. I shiver whenever I think of taking him out in public and tremble when I think of being alone with him.

Last week, I drove him downtown for lunch. One of my old friends, Danielle Lafontaine, was walking by with her nine-year-old granddaughter. She saw us sitting out on the sidewalk terrace and stopped to say *bonjour*. We hadn't talked in a long time, and I wasn't sure how much she knew about Saul's condition, but the hesitant smile and quick kiss on his cheek answered the question.

Saul looked up at her and over at the little girl and started spewing the "F" word. Danielle grabbed her granddaughter's hand and rushed away.

That wasn't the first time he'd sworn like that in public, and Dr. Tremblay told me it probably wouldn't be the last. But I can't exactly hang a sign around his neck saying *Alzheimer's patient*, so what am I supposed to do?

If it were just that, I could probably handle it. What really scares me is being alone with him. There are things I haven't shared with you, the children, or anyone else. They were too humiliating. But I have to tell someone.

A few days ago, he walked into the kitchen naked and began to masturbate. I told him in a firm voice that his behavior was unacceptable. He called me Gisele and told me he was going to give it to me. Suddenly, he turned me around and raised my dress. I tried to fight him off, but he was too strong. He ripped my apron and then my dress, and we both tumbled to the floor. Then a few moments later, he pushed himself up on his knees, stood up, and left the room as if nothing had happened.

The next day, he started wandering around the house, calling my name. I told him I was there. He glanced at me with a blank look and asked me if I had seen Monique.

I said, "I am Monique."

He continued walking through the house, calling for me. I followed him to make sure he didn't hurt himself. I had already installed special latches on the cabinets, security locks on the windows, and hung chimes on the outside doors so I would know if he left the house, but I was still afraid he would find a way to hurt himself.

When he got to our bedroom, he turned around and slapped me in the face, pushed me to the floor, jumped on top of me, and started punching my stomach. Moments later, as I lay on the carpet covered in my own vomit, he knelt beside me, stroked my hair, and asked me why I was crying.

Dr. Tremblay had told me that Saul might get violent, but I wasn't expecting this. I know I am supposed to be sympathetic, but that's getting harder and harder. I am about to go off the deep end.

The next morning, I called Joey and Florence. I couldn't bring myself to tell them what had happened that night or any other night, nor will I ever. I just said things were getting worse and muttered my way through the conversations without mentioning any of the horrific details. We all agreed it was time. In fact, both children had told me months ago that it was time. So I called Manoir Laurier to find out if they still had rooms available. When I'd visited there two months ago, I'd found it more like a senior citizen's home than a place where awful people like me abandon their spouses. That made me feel somewhat better.

JOEY
AM I SCREWED?

Yesterday, I went to my doctor, who told me that there are genes you inherit that can tell if you are predisposed to Alzheimer's. I'd never heard of that. I asked if there was a test, and he said yes, but they don't do it in Quebec, because if the results are bad, a person might think of doing something untoward. I assume he meant suicide.

Well, I'm not going to hang around and wait. I'll go down to the States and get tested if I have to. I can handle whatever the results may be, but I can't handle the uncertainty of not knowing whether there is a time bomb ticking in my body that is already eating away at my brain.

I watch my old man, a tough prick if there ever was one—cold, indifferent, distant, not much of a father, frankly—turning into a lapdog. You know, they say that what goes around comes around. In his case, he must be paying for how he treated not only me but Mother, as well. She was the quintessential doormat, and now she rules the roost. In a way, I figure she must secretly be enjoying the power she wields. She tells him what to wear, what to eat, when to go to sleep, and he can't so much as utter a peep about it—and if he does, my guess is that she blows him off and does what she wants anyway. Frankly, given what she's been through all these years, I'm not sure I blame her. Ah, revenge is sweet!

I'm pissed off that he may have passed on the bad genes to me. I mean, I know that part's not his fault, but I kind of feel that not only has he not been there for me but that as a last act he may have dealt me the early-death card. And maybe Florence has the bad genes, too, and may pass them on to her boys.

SAUL
CUSTER'S LAST STAND

That's what I'm acting out now, trying to keep up appearances, trying to fool the last Indians sneaking up on me. And it is becoming more than wearisome. In fact, it's becoming practically impossible.

I'm not sure, but I think I told you about the blackboard, the one where I can see things, but sometimes I can't say them like they're written on the board. Well, now it's even hard for me to read the blackboard, let alone tell you what it says. It's sort of okay at this moment—a bit jumbled, but I can make out most of it.

Before, I could think rationally for good amounts of time and talk to you like I am now. Those hours of clarity are turning into minutes, and will eventually be seconds, and then just a dark, empty hole. The times of going until sundown in a fairly normal state are all but—I was going to say a fading memory, but then you would think, Well—duh—he's crazy! But I am not crazy, just one of the millions of unlucky winners of a worldwide lottery that will eventually reduce me to ashes.

I say ashes because that is what I am requesting in the letter I am composing right now. But it is so hard to write anymore. Do you see those crumpled balls of white paper lying on the floor? They're from my frustration at not being able to join the letters that once were the best letters anyone ever wrote. That's what Mrs. Trautman told me in the seventh grade. In fact, she said I would probably be a . . . calligraf . . . something—damn, I am getting tired of not being able to find the words I want. And the more tired I get, the harder it is. The point I am trying to make is that as I put the words down on paper, they don't always look like what I meant to write.

I already told you I have a will, and it's down at Friedman's office. The thing I'm writing today is a cod . . . ah . . . cod . . . codicil—yes, that's the word! When I get a word, especially a big one like that, I feel like my mother should appear with a double-chocolate Howard Johnson's ice-cream cone as a reward. There would be no worry of my gaining weight, because I don't get that many words right, as you have probably guessed by now; besides, there's not that much time left.

My mother is gone. It was really pathetic watching her waste away. Toward the end, her face looked like a spider colony from smoking those foul cigarettes.

I am asking Monique and the children not to have a funeral service. Just to take my body up to the crematorium. I don't want anyone to open my casket. Just let them lower the box into the stove, or whatever it is, and get it over with. I don't want them to hang around until the flames cut through the wood and start licking my body.

I am almost as good as gone right now. I sometimes pray God will speed things up. No Manoir Laurier, no Belfrage Hospital—just straight to the cemetery—like in that game where you go directly to jail without collecting your two hundred dollars.

I can count on the children to bury my ashes beside Mother, Father, and Miriam. It will probably be sad for them because they will see there are places for them, and, of course, for Monique.

I have a confession to make. I didn't really tell you the whole truth about the funeral stuff. The fact is, I am worried that very few people will show up. I was never Mr. Popularity, and being kind of a hermit, I haven't kept up with whatever friends I had, if indeed they were friends at all. I don't want to embarrass my family. I can just see the chapel at Silverberg and Sons—empty except for a few souls scattered in the back rows. In the Jewish religion, the immediate family sits off to the side so they can weep in peace without everyone seeing them. I'm not sure they would need much Kleenex at my funeral.

I once heard Alzheimer's called "the disease of many farewells," so named because we slide further and further down the slippery slope to darkness, with no chance of recovery. But I have already given up on any chance of recovery.

For me, Alzheimer's is just a slow dance with death. Soon I won't know who I am or where I am. But Monique and the others will. I want to spare them the trouble of taking care of me or visiting me in an institution. And I want to spare myself the humiliation of being bathed, fed, and having my diaper changed—even though I may not know what is happening.

But today Monique told me everything would be all right, and that she would be there for me. And who knows, she said in an absent voice, maybe they'll find a cure.

After she said that, I reluctantly found my way to my den and pulled that book out from under a stack of magazines. I had written myself a note and left it on my desk, telling me where the book was in case I forgot. I tossed it in the trash out back, and with it, my suicide plan. Now I'm in it for the long haul. But in my case, I guess the term *long* is relative.

MONIQUE
THE CRUISE

Saul and I love the ocean. We have probably been on more than twenty cruises over the years. So I figured that if there was anywhere for us to spend what would most certainly be our last holiday together before he goes to Manoir Laurier, it should be on the water.

Bernie and Florence said they had to take care of their kids, and Joey said he was still trying to get his business up and running. That left Saul and me to go alone, not something that made me happy. I was afraid that he would have one of his tantrums—or even worse.

After the episode with my friend Danielle and her granddaughter, which I shared with you, you're probably thinking, Why on earth would she take him on a cruise, of all things? Well, it probably wasn't the smartest idea, but I thought that this was about Saul. Some final pleasure, if it wasn't too late already. And if I could do that for him, then it would all be worth it.

I chose the *Constellation Mariner* because we had sailed on it three or four times, and Saul might not feel as lost as he would on a ship he had never sailed on. I decided to hire a male nurse who had been recommended to me, as it was becoming more difficult to help Saul get around. And frankly, because I yearned for some adult conversation and company.

When the young man came to our door for his interview I knew right away that he was the one. He had olive-brown skin that contrasted with his crisp white shirt, and a pleasant face with deep-set chestnut eyes. It turned out that he was from Lebanon and had been trained as an anesthesiologist over there. He couldn't get certified in Quebec without going back to school for three years, something he couldn't afford to do. It's sad when someone else's problems become our good fortune, but better that than the other way around, I suppose. Saul and I had enough misery already.

The trip from Montreal to Miami was easy. Amin wheeled Saul through the airport and onto the plane, then strapped him into the seat beside me. At the other end, a porter was waiting with another wheelchair and got us to a limo I had arranged, and we were off to Port Everglades, in Fort Lauderdale.

As we turned the corner after the security checkpoint, the ship came into view. I could see the look on Saul's face, like that of a child who was seeing his first towering vessel. He pressed his face against the window and his eyes widened. Then he turned toward me and smiled. I wondered if he somehow knew this was going to be his last vacation.

Our cabin was one of the larger suites, located on deck ten. I chose that one because it had an oversize balcony, big enough to maneuver the wheelchair *Constellation* provided. Although Saul used a wheelchair at home only occasionally, I thought with the motion of the sea and the long corridors, it would be easier. Amin was in an adjoining room, so that I wouldn't have to go out into the hallway in the middle of the night if I needed him.

The first evening, I decided that Amin should roll Saul to the dining room on deck five, as it would be easier to leave him in the wheelchair than to move him into one of the chairs at the table by the window.

Saul had his own plan. He said he wanted to sit in one of the chairs. I made the mistake of telling him he should stay where he was. Next thing I knew, he bellowed and then swept his long arm over the table, leaving only a few plates and two water glasses standing, and a big mess on the taupe carpet. My face turned scarlet. I was petrified to turn around, wondering how many diners had witnessed his tantrum. It's one thing when your friends know about his condition, or when you won't see people again, but I had nine more nights to suffer through and excuses to make. I could feel the heat of hundreds of eyes boring into my back as I watched Amin and the waiters quickly clean up the mess.

We managed to get through dinner without another incident. Saul sat in a dining room chair between Amin and me, and we both helped him with his food. I drank a little too much and now know how dizzy Saul must feel every night.

Saul said he wanted to walk back to the suite, and I certainly wasn't going to argue with him. It took almost half an hour, as he kept stopping and talking to both real and imaginary people. I was sure by now that everyone on the ship had either seen or heard about the crazy man and his entourage.

There was another incident I want to share with you. One day—I think it was about halfway into the cruise—we were sitting alone on the deck outside the Globe Lounge at teatime. Amin had secured the wheels on Saul's wheelchair and left us alone so he could get some well-deserved time off. I placed a straw in the iced tea and put the glass within Saul's reach. He picked it up, put the straw in his mouth, and took a big sip. Then he put the glass back on the table, but he didn't release his hand. Seconds later, he picked up the glass and drank again. This went on until the tea was drained. Then he stared at the empty glass for a moment and proceeded to pick it up and try to drink again. He did this over and over.

I told him there was nothing left and that he should put the glass down. He just looked through me. I told him again. He turned to me and smiled as he smashed the glass against the table. Then he picked up a large shard and sliced it across his arm, drawing a red river of blood.

I must have shrieked loudly enough to wake up all the sea life below. Two waiters raced outside. One grabbed the piece of glass from Saul's hand, cutting himself in the process; the other one rushed back into the lounge, heading toward a telephone by the bar.

Moments later, Amin came flying through the door, followed by a young woman in a nurse's uniform. He took Saul's arm and wiped it with a napkin. Then Amin examined it and used the napkin as a tourniquet. He told the nurse that Saul had missed the artery but said they should move him down to the infirmary on deck three to get him stitched up.

Thank God the rest of the trip was normal—well, as normal as could be expected under the circumstances. But, you know, all in all—for Saul's sake—I'm glad we went. And to be fair, there were some good moments—really good ones. Like when we were at the captain's cocktail party and the band was playing a song Saul knew. He harmonized in a very quiet voice, forgetting most of the words, but with a glint in his eyes and just a slight hint of a wink and a smile as he turned to look at me. Or when we were watching a few couples dance to the band after dinner one night. He was in his wheelchair, but he looked over at me and in a clear voice asked me to dance. Before I could even figure out how to respond, his gaze slipped back to the floor, and he retreated into his own world. But just for that moment, a brief one at that, it was like it used to be when we cruised together. And moments like that made it all worth it.

MONIQUE
NO CHOICE

The first few days after the trip were without incident—more or less. But that changed suddenly. In the last week, there was a beating, which resulted in a bruised arm and a cut on my left cheek. If that wasn't bad enough, he used disgusting language, and I mean really disgusting.

The beating came out of thin air. He just got up and hit me. Thank God I was able to cover my face. After a few attempts to pry my arms away, he seemed satisfied to push me and slap my shoulders a few times before he calmed down. I can't go through this anymore. Not for another month, another week, or even another day.

Joey, Florence, and Bernie are coming over later this afternoon. I have been packing Saul's things all day. The administrator at Manoir Laurier told me to bring a few pairs of pajamas in addition to his clothes, and Velcro running shoes, which would be easier to put on and take off. Loose-fitting clothes, she said, would be more comfortable, especially when he has to be confined to a wheelchair. Just hearing her say that set me off crying again.

It is beginning to dawn on me that the man I have lived with for all these years is leaving me for good tonight. Never to step foot in our house again. Never to put his strong arm around my back, or throw his long leg over mine as we fall asleep. Never to fill the kitchen with the aroma of his coffee in the morning. It is as if he is heading to the execution chamber.

Part of me is relieved and part of me is scared, very scared. Why can't we just go back in time? It's true it hasn't been a perfect marriage, but we've had a decent life together. And we have two children and two wonderful grandchildren. Maybe I should have been more appreciative of what we did have together. Sometimes I ask myself what gave me the right to judge him? Did I do what I could in this marriage? So many questions and so few answers. But I guess I will have lots of time to think about them. Lots of time to reminisce. Lots of loneliness.

DR. TREMBLAY
INEVITABLE

You were doubtless thinking that I was referring to Mr. Reimer. And you probably said to yourself, I know there is no cure, and death is inevitable. And Mr. Reimer will be no exception.

No, I was referring to whether his son, Joey, may follow in his father's footsteps. He came to my office last Wednesday, armed with a manila envelope that contained the results of a blood test he had done down in Vermont. The test is frowned upon in Quebec, and when it is performed for research purposes, the results are usually confidential and kept from the patient.

The lab had sealed the envelope, and as far as I could tell, Joey had not opened it. He asked me to take a look at it and tell him what it meant. As he passed it over to me, I could see the perspiration forming on his brow. I offered him a seat and then returned to my desk, sat back in my leather chair, and slid a letter opener under the flap. I looked down at the beige paper with a neat letterhead in block letters at the top. The lab had performed a test on chromosome 19 to discover more about the apolipoprotein gene.

Let me explain what they were looking for, and what that means to someone like Joey. The protein known as apolipoprotein, or ApoE, comes in three possible varieties: 2, 3, and 4. All of them help the body deliver cholesterol and triglyceride fats to cells through the bloodstream. We inherit one copy of the gene from our mother and one copy from our father.

The ApoE2 gene is the most efficient and generally protects us from Alzheimer's. If you have two ApoE2 genes you could probably smoke a pack of cigarettes a day, drink a quart of vodka, and skip the gym—all with relatively no ill effects, although I am not recommending you do that.

The most common gene is ApoE3, which means we have to watch our diet, exercise, and generally maintain a healthy lifestyle. ApoE4 is the least efficient in doing its job, and although not an absolute predictor of Alzheimer's, it means we are four times more likely to get the disease if we have one copy, and ten times more likely if we inherit two copies.

Still, we don't do this kind of testing for two reasons: First, there are some people who have one ApoE4 gene, or even two, who don't go on to develop Alzheimer's. Second, other than for research purposes, it makes no sense, in my opinion, to burden people with the fact that the odds are that they may succumb to the disease, when there is no cure.

Sure, there are some doctors, especially in the United States, who think a patient has a right to know everything about his body and his health. They are the same ones who order the spinal tap or a PET scan looking at amyloid buildup. I am not one of those, nor are most of my fellow doctors in Canada. And for that reason, I did not even mention these tests to Joey.

Joey's eyes were glued on me, searching for any sign of reassurance. I removed my glasses and looked at the blurry form in front of me.

He said, "Well? What do you think?"

I said, "These tests serve no purpose, and it's best just to let me pass on the results for research purposes."

He said, "I really want to know. Let's do this now."

I put my glasses back on and could see his face flushed, more with fear than anger.

I glanced once more at the sheet of paper in front of me and then looked up and said, "Unfortunately, you have two copies of the ApoE4 gene."

FLORENCE
WHAT IF?

Joey came over today. A rare visit. He knows Bernie and I aren't going to lend him any more money. He's already in hock to us for over thirty thousand dollars. Bernie says to forget ever seeing any of it again, but somehow I think Joey will make it eventually. Or maybe it's just blind hope for him.

He marched in, brushing by me like a man on a mission. I thought he would sit down when he got to the living room, but he just kept circling the furniture. I could tell this was a big one. What it was, I wasn't sure, and something told me I didn't want to know.

He didn't waste any time getting to the reason for his visit. He had been to Dr. Tremblay, he explained, and the doctor had told him he had two copies of the ApoE4 gene. Even though I had no idea what he was talking about, I knew it wasn't good. And I was right.

By the time Joey finished explaining what it meant, my body was covered in goose bumps. Joey, my only brother, might end up like Father. He tried to put up a front of bravado, but I could see the fear in his eyes. I told him I would be there for him, and his slight nod told me he knew I would be.

Then he asked about me. What if I had this ApoE4 gene, or, worse, two of them? Suddenly, it dawned on me. It wasn't just about Joey; it was about me, as well. My life as I knew it could change one day on a dime. I, too, could end up like my father.

After a few seconds of digesting all this, I realized this wasn't even just about Joey and me; it was about my kids. If I had even one copy, my kids could inherit it. And if, God forbid, Bernie had one, too, the kids could have two copies—according to Joey, an almost certain death sentence.

If I had the test and didn't have the gene—fine. But what if I did? What would I do next? Have Bernie tested? Have the kids tested? And what if I did all that and the results weren't what I wanted to hear? Then what? What could I do, anyway, other than worry? According to Dr. Tremblay, there is no cure on the horizon.

Joey and I both agreed that I should tell Bernie, but with Mother's frail health, it would be better not to say anything to her.

Bernie nearly had a breakdown when I told him. But I reasoned, Look, maybe I have a copy, or even two; maybe I don't. And even if I do, it's not a sure thing that I would get it, so why not just let it be. As for the kids, given their age, I'm sure even if all this came to be, there would be a cure by that time. Or would there?

PART THREE
THE FINAL STOP

MONIQUE
DAY 1—MANOIR LAURIER

It was like a procession tonight as we pulled up to the Manoir. Three cars—Saul and I in a taxi, followed by Florence and Bernie, and Joey's noisy sports car in the rear.

I looked through the window at what seemed like a typical hotel dining room. At eight o'clock, it was already empty. As was the lobby, with its marble entry, high-back chairs covered in somber-colored chintz, and mahogany furniture sitting on a beautiful circular rug.

The first set of glass doors opened automatically. But the second set wouldn't open until the first closed, and I had to push a little black button near the top of the door. I guess this complicated process kept the patients safely inside. A pudgy middle-aged woman with too much perfume came out from behind a small desk to the right where there were several screens showing different parts of the building. We exchanged a few pleasantries, and then she took Saul's arm and signaled for me to follow.

The three of us waited for the elevator while the kids went to get Saul's things from Bernie's car. I remembered that when I'd come here the first time to tour the facility, the administrator had told me that there were no rooms on the first floor, except for the dining room, kitchen, offices, and some large rooms for communal activities. The second floor, she said, was for elderly patients with less serious illnesses.

When the elevator opened, a rotund man in pajamas and a bathrobe was standing at the back. The woman asked him where he was going. The man smiled and replied, "To the swimming pool." The woman smiled back. And that was it.

I said, "I didn't know there was a swimming pool."

The woman smiled again, but this time at me. "That's right," she said, "there is no swimming pool."

Saul didn't seem to understand exactly what was happening. On the way over, I'd tried to reassure him that he would like it here, and that it wouldn't be permanent. I hated myself for lying to him, but I didn't have the resolve to tell him he would never sleep in his own house again.

When I'd gone over earlier to sign the necessary papers, the administrator had told me we could furnish Saul's room in any way we wanted. The kids and I had decided right then that we would pack up as many things as we could to decorate his new room so that he will be in somewhat familiar surroundings, and, hopefully, be less agitated.

Joey will rent a U-Haul tomorrow. We'll fill it with some bedroom furniture, family pictures, and his favorite chair. That's the least we can do.

The elevator stopped on the fourth floor. It holds twenty-six Alzheimer's patients in the middle stage of the disease. The third floor is reserved for those closer to death. Well, if this was the middle stage, I dreaded to see what would come next.

I almost collided with an emaciated woman walking in the pink-colored hallway, squeezing the sides of her nightgown while chirping like a bird. Directly behind her, a man groaned in a voice that sounded like the devil himself. My first reaction was to grab

Saul and head back home. I guess the woman with the heavy per-fume must have realized how uneasy I was. She reached over and touched my arm.

The room was small, maybe twelve by eighteen feet, with a bathroom and a tiny closet. The walls were bare, the floor was lino-leum, and the bed had side rails. As elegant as the lobby was, the room forced me to come to grips with the fact that this was no more than a fancy hospital.

SAUL

DAY 2—WHERE AM I?

When I woke up this morning, my head felt like it was stuffed with cotton. I looked out the window. The Brodskys' house wasn't there anymore. They must have moved it in the middle of the night. I put my blue-checkered robe over my pajamas and headed into the kitchen like I always do, but it wasn't there, either. In its place was some kind of lounge with couches and chairs. I guess if they could move a house, they could certainly move a kitchen!

I hollered for Monique, but she didn't answer. So I started searching for her. The house just didn't seem the same. For one thing, I never would have let Monique paint the hallways pink. That's for sure. It's enough that I let her get away with it in the bedroom.

Some lady came over to me, put her hand on my arm, and asked me if I was okay.

"Hell no!" I said. "How can I be okay when someone moved the kitchen and repainted the hallway?"

She smiled at me. Kind of the same smile Friedman always doled out, but she was much prettier than Friedman. She took my hand and started leading me back toward my bedroom. I yanked it away, almost knocking her to the floor in the process. I picked up steam as I came to the end of the corridor and rushed into an open elevator. But we don't have an elevator in the house. I pushed the lowest button, and a few moments later, when the doors opened, I was in a big room with fancy furniture and a glass wall that looked out onto a garden. I must have walked into the wrong house!

I went over to a woman sitting at a desk by the front door and apologized for barging in. She, too, gave me the Friedman smile.

Then something snapped in my head, and I realized I had no idea where I was, but it wasn't at home with Monique. And wherever I was, I was all alone. I sank down to the cold marble floor and began to cry.

MONIQUE
DAY 2—WHAT'S HAPPENING?

I didn't sleep the whole night. I kept reaching out for Saul. Finally, I got myself out of bed, took a hot shower, and headed down the hill to see him.

The autumn air was cold, but I decided to walk instead of taking a taxi. Part of me wanted to get there as soon as possible, but another part, frankly, never wanted to get there at all.

The first set of glass doors opened, and I waited as they closed behind me. For a moment, it felt like I, too, was imprisoned, stuck between the two doors, trapped, just like Saul upstairs. I pushed the black button on the wall, and the second set of doors opened. I inhaled a deep breath of air and made my way through the lobby to the elevator.

When I got upstairs, I went down the hall to Saul's room. He wasn't there. I panicked. Horrible thoughts filled my mind. Had he escaped? Was he dead? What would I tell the children? How could I live knowing I would never see him again?

I heard voices behind me, one of them familiar.

"What are you doing here?" Saul asked. "I told you I don't want the room done until after lunch."

I turned and smiled, holding my arms out. Then he told me he had no intention of sleeping with me, that I was just a cheap whore. Besides, he said, Monique would be home any minute.

The nurse patted his arm, saying, "Mr. Reimer, this is your wife."

He said, "Of course," and then kissed me on the cheek before walking into his room.

The nurse told me I could take him to the dining room for breakfast, that it was okay as long as the residents could eat by themselves, or with a caregiver. *Mon Dieu*, I have gone from a wife to a mother over many years, and now from a wife and mother to a caregiver in only two days!

She said once the residents deteriorated to the point where it wasn't possible to eat in the dining room anymore, they would have to eat in the third-floor lounge, where there was more supervision and where the staff could help feed them. And when things got worse, they would have to have their meals in their rooms. I can barely cope with today, let alone allowing myself to imagine Saul ending up worse than those crazies we saw last night.

There were only a few people in the dining room. One elderly lady sat at a table by a large window that overlooked the quiet residential street, chewing the same piece of food over and over again, while her private nurse waited to give her the next spoonful. Another woman wandered between the tables until one of the servers took hold of her arm and guided her back to her seat.

I chose a table in the corner by a fake palm tree. Saul pulled my chair out and waited until I sat down before doing so himself. He seemed not to notice that he was in this new milieu. He asked me about the kids, wanting to know whether Joey's business was doing okay yet and whether Florence would be stopping by to see him. I can't figure all this out. It's like sometimes he's here and sometimes he's not, like in that television program *The Twilight Zone*.

The dining room was much like that of a typical Sheraton hotel. For a moment, it was as if Saul and I were having breakfast on one of our trips. Except there was no newspaper in front of Saul's face. We used to travel a lot, until he became more and more reluctant to leave home. I didn't know it then, but I know now that not wanting to leave familiar surroundings is an early sign of Alzheimer's. I wonder if he would be any better off today if I had recognized it back then.

A spindly waitress in a gray uniform brought over two plates heaped with scrambled eggs and placed them in front of us.

I said, "My husband absolutely detests scrambled eggs and will never eat them. Can he have something else?"

As she rattled off the other choices, I looked over at Saul, who had a vacant smile on his face, and was shoveling the last of the eggs into his mouth. I hardly know this man anymore, I thought.

SAUL
DAY 2—GOOD FOOD

Went to a new foOd place with Monique.
Really good. We're goiNg back next tiMe.

SAUL
DAY 33—THE POLICE

To the best of my recollection, I have never called 911—until today. But when it comes to murder—my own murder—I had no choice. There is some kind of conspiracy to keep me here against my will and assassinate me. It's the same group who were responsible for John Lennon's death and the attempt on Ronald Reagan's life. They've now moved north into Canada, and I am their first intended victim. I suspected something when they began following me every time I left the house. They never spoke directly to me. They didn't have to. I knew they were after me.

I just got off the phone with Sergeant Lacolle. The others I spoke to before him asked for my address and phone number and said they would send a car, but no one ever showed up. So finally, I asked for a supervisor and got this Lacolle guy. He seemed to be familiar with my case. I asked him when the police were going to come for me, and if I should hide until they arrived. As I said that, I looked around the room and told the sergeant there was no real closet, just a shallow thing stuck on the wall. I asked if I should hide in the bathroom. He said that really wasn't necessary.

I asked him how many police cars there would be.

He said, "At least two."

I said, "That's good, because there are probably a lot of bad guys."

He asked me if I would be okay until then. I told him it was hard to tell, because if those same guys who were holding me here against my will got through the barricade I had set up against the door, there was no telling what they might do. He said his officers were on their way and should be here in a moment.

I told him I heard loud banging on my door. He said that must be his men and that I should remove the barricade and let them in.

I said, "What if it's not your men?"

He said he was sure. And he was a policeman—not only a policeman—but a sergeant.

So I laid the receiver on the table and moved the bureau away from the door.

Sergeant Lacolle is a liar.

MONIQUE
DAY 185—MUSIC

Saul was sitting in his favorite chair, dressed in a polo shirt and cardigan sweater, gazing out the window—watching nothing. He looked up and smiled when he heard the door bang against the wall as it opened. I pulled out a container of yogurt from my bag and asked him if he wanted any. "No, never," he said. So I put it in the small fridge by the bathroom and took a seat in the brown leather chair opposite him.

"How are you feeling today?" I asked.

"How are you feeling today?" he repeated.

"Did you have a good sleep?" I asked.

"Sleep," he said.

And that's how it went for the few minutes we spent together, until one of the orderlies came in to remind me that they were having a sing-along in the lounge. I asked Saul if he wanted to go downstairs and spend some time with the other residents. He stood up without answering. I took him by the arm and guided him toward the elevator.

The lounge was full when we arrived. There were tables covered in red plastic lined up neatly across the room. Most of the residents were in wheelchairs, many of them slouching forward, their eyes closed. I guess they were the zombies from the third floor.

We took a seat on a bench in the back. A young woman, maybe twenty-five years old, with straight blond hair down to her waist, was singing and playing an acoustic guitar that was hanging from her neck on a bright yellow cord. Saul seemed more interested in checking out the others in the room than in watching her.

In a way, I'm glad we waited this long to bring him here, because he would be mortified if he knew he was in a room with people who were so far gone. He is one of the sanest here. No, that's not the word I mean. He is one of those who are not yet in the final stages of the disease. Sometimes, when I think of that, I feel blessed that I will have him around longer. But then I look around at some of the others and realize that he will end up just like them. And then I think, What will it be like for him? And what will it be like for me?

The young woman handed out tambourines to a few of the residents and began singing "When the Saints Go Marching In." She stopped in front of a man who held one of the tambourines in his hand. He was just staring at it. She took it from him and started banging on it. The man smiled as she handed it back to him, and she watched as he hit the tambourine against the table. Then he began to sing the words out loud, a huge grin on his face, like a child who had done something he was proud of. The woman moved on, cajoling many of those in the room to join her as she played one song after another.

The man beside me seemed comatose until she sang in French. Then his eyes opened and his head bobbed from side to side. When she started singing in English again, he went back to wherever he had been.

As she approached Saul, he stood up, ever the gentleman, even in his state. She began to sing "Shine on Harvest Moon." Saul put his arm around her shoulder and started harmonizing. He had been a member of a barbershop quartet for years, and that was his favorite song. Saul may be—what's that expression?—down on the canvas—but don't count him out yet.

SAUL

DAY 185—THE BARBERSHOP

Went to the barBers today with . . . you
know . . . the one with the kNockers . . .
Sang the moOn song. It was fuN.

JOEY
DAY 197—SCARY

You have to hear this. I went to see Dad today. He was sitting in the small lounge by the elevator on the fourth floor, talking to another patient. From what I could tell, they were speaking mostly gibberish. So I walk up to him—and you have to believe me on this one—and say, "Yo, Pops, what's going on?"

He stands up, takes my elbow, and motions me back toward the elevator. Then in a firm voice he says, "Look, I'm in a meeting now. Would you mind coming back later?"

I did everything in my power not to break out laughing. It was amazing. I'm not making fun of him or anything. I mean—come on—he's my father, for Christ's sake! But some of the things that come out of his mouth now . . .

And wait, it gets better. When I left—which, by the way, was not when he told me to leave, because within a few seconds he had forgotten that he even said it—I hailed a taxi at the front entrance.

As a deliveryman was leaving the side entrance, a woman dressed in a bathrobe came flying past him out the door and grabbed me through the open window of the cab.

"Son," she said, "please don't leave me here. I promise to behave. Let me come back home."

I was floored. And frankly, I didn't know what to do or say. Thank God a nurse rushed out, corralled her, and guided her back into the building—but not before the woman pleaded again for me to take her with me.

I closed the window of the taxi and gave the driver the address of the garage where my car was being serviced. The cabbie didn't say a word until we got there. Then he turned around and hissed, "You should be ashamed of yourself. How could you treat your mother that way?"

I said, "She's not my mother."

He said, "Just get out of my cab. You disgust me."

It was obvious I wasn't going to change his mind, so I just threw the fare on the front seat and slammed the door. You couldn't make this stuff up if you tried.

MONIQUE
DAY 217—DINNER FOR TWO

I never want to see this place again. It's bad enough when I'm home alone at night, thinking about all the terrible things that must be going on here, but to be here and witness them myself—it's criminal!

Sometimes I wish Saul would have killed himself when he was first diagnosed. It would have saved him from this miserable existence, and saved the children and me from our unbearable agony.

Today was awful. I'm told it will get even worse, but I can't imagine how. I was late—I usually like to get there before lunch so that I can help Saul with his food. It isn't that the people on the staff aren't good, but there just aren't enough of them to give the personal attention I want for him.

When I reached the fourth-floor lounge, an elegant lady with snow-white coiffed hair, dressed in a silk suit with a fancy silver broach, was sitting erect at one end of a long banquet table covered with blue-and-white-checkered plastic. Saul sat at the other end, in his polo shirt, hunched over. They were the only two at the table. The scene reminded me of one of those dinners between a husband and wife in a European castle, where they were so far apart that they couldn't hear each other talk—and probably preferred it that way.

Saul was quite agitated. Wouldn't you be, having to suffer like he is? He was banging on his plate with his spoon, softly at first, and then louder, as if building up to a grand crescendo. One of the staff took the spoon from his hand. He picked up his fork and started banging again. Suddenly, the woman at the other end of the table shouted at him to shut up and stuck her tongue out.

The others in the lounge didn't even look up. But Saul did, and he started to bang louder and louder. Now the woman was on her feet, furious, waving her fist at Saul with such ferocity that I was scared she was going to go over and punch him. The orderlies didn't seem concerned—all in a day's work, I guess.

The woman continued shaking her fist and called him a bastard, yelling that his teeth would fly if he didn't shut up. Then she began using the "F" word, saying she was going to f—ing kill him if he didn't shut up. Well, let me tell you, I would have f—ing killed her if she'd gotten any closer to him.

This went on for just a few moments—Saul banging, and the woman threatening him. Then, just as quickly as it started, it stopped, and it was as if nothing had happened.

SAUL
DAY 217—THE WOMAN

biTchy! BitCh!

MONIQUE
DAY 231—JUST ANOTHER DAY AT THE MANOIR

Do you remember the lady who sat across from Saul at the lunch table a couple of weeks ago? The one who threatened him because she didn't like him banging his fork? Well, today when I arrived at the Manoir just after noon, there she was, sitting in her same spot. One of the attendants told me that she causes a big scene if anyone tries to take her place at the head of the table. Another woman was seated beside her, also dressed to the nines. They seemed to be caught up in very serious conversation. You would think they were solving the world's problems. But when I moved closer, I realized that neither one was saying anything coherent, in French or English.

The other chairs were occupied by an assortment of loonies. I'm sorry. I don't mean that, but sometimes I really believe that all these people are so much further gone than Saul, that their behavior is rubbing off on him, propelling him quickly down the abyss. Look at him sitting over there, oblivious to me or any of the others. That's not the way he was when he arrived here. And look at that Italian guy chewing his food over and over. It reminds me of when I went to a spa years ago. They taught us it was healthy to chew every piece of food twenty times before swallowing. This guy must be doing it a hundred times. It will be dinnertime before he finishes lunch.

And look at the man beside him, whistling through his false teeth. The sound is driving me crazy. And the woman who seems to have hijacked her fellow diners' orange juice cans and keeps moving them around like some kind of shell game. Other than that old witch and her friend, none of them is even talking to any of the others, let alone aware of the others' presence.

I must be honest with you. I am torn about coming down here, but I do come every day. The kids haven't been pulling their weight. Well, that's not really fair. Florence has been here a lot, considering her work and that she has to be there for Howard and Daniel. And she always brings some of Saul's favorite foods, although he doesn't seem to remember he likes them.

I guess its Joey I'm upset with. Sure, he shows up a couple of times a week. But he lives less than ten blocks away and only stays for a few minutes. He spends more time with that damn dog than he does with his own father. The social worker downstairs said maybe he can't face the thought that his father is dying. I frankly think he just doesn't really care that much, and that this whole thing is cramping his style. He'd rather be out with his friends than be here with his family. I must say I am disappointed, more than disappointed.

The head nurse on Saul's floor told me that he has been acting up at night, and they have been giving him some drugs to calm him down. I guess that's okay, and maybe the drugs make whatever time he has more pleasant. He deserves that.

JOEY
DAY 242—DOG DAY AFTERNOON

Mother has always hated him, and Florence claims Bernie is allergic to cats and dogs. So ever since Dad was admitted to Manoir Laurier, I have become Dugin's guardian.

Let me get one thing straight: I'm no dog lover. But having shared that with you, I felt an obligation to take Dugin in, knowing how much he means to Dad.

They don't let dogs into Manoir Laurier, even for visits. So if it's a nice day and I can get away from my work for a while—which, I must admit, isn't often—I take Dad out for a walk with Dugin. They still have a connection, that's for sure. Even when Dad is in a foul mood or not totally with the program, his face lights up when he sees Dugin. And the feeling is obviously mutual. You can tell that by how Dugin drools and wags his tail.

What drives me crazy is the hair he sheds all over my black suede sofa. That's where I usually start my pitch to the ladies—you know, a couple of glasses of chardonnay, some kissing and fondling, and then into the bedroom for the grand finale. At least that's the way it used to be. Now the chicks look at the scuzzy gold hair and won't go near the couch.

I ordered a new leather one from a discount outlet, but it won't be here for another couple of weeks. And now it looks like it won't really matter by then.

You're probably asking yourself, Why won't it matter? Well, Dugin was vomiting a lot last week and didn't seem to have much energy. So a few days ago, I took him down to Dr. Nelson's office. He examined him and did some tests, blood work, and an X-ray. He called me the next day and informed me that Dugin has liver cancer.

I told Mom. She reacted like I had just mentioned I had a headache. And it didn't play much better with Florence. Both of them told me I was nuts to worry about a mutt when Dad was going through so much. Maybe reality is they're both feeling sorry for themselves for what they're going through.

Regardless, I wasn't going to let Dugin suffer, so I called Dr. Nelson and told him we all agreed—I was too embarrassed to tell him my mother and sister didn't give a shit—that Dugin should be put down.

This afternoon, I took Dugin to Dr. Nelson's. The receptionist showed us into a room with a table in the middle. Dr. Nelson came in a few minutes later. He reached down and placed both hands around Dugin's face and told him he would be fine and then hoisted him onto the table. He asked me if I wanted Dugin buried or cremated. Good question. What would Dad want? Not that it really matters, I guess, because he won't know anyway. Or will he? I often wonder how much, if anything, he does understand. Dr. Tremblay said even in his condition, maybe a fair amount. Not all the time, that's for sure, but probably more than we think.

I told the doctor to have him cremated and give me back the ashes. When Dad goes, I'll place the urn beside his at the cemetery. That's what he would probably want.

Dr. Nelson started preparing the syringe. Dugin lay in front of me. I thought I saw him grimace for a moment, and then he stopped, almost as if he wasn't going to let anyone know he was in pain. It was obvious he had been suffering quite a bit the past few days. I could see it in his eyes, which had turned a muddy yellow, and the way he could barely lift himself up on the sofa.

Dr. Nelson put his hand on my shoulder and told me to take whatever time I needed to say good-bye, and then he started toward the open door to his private office. I almost called out, "I don't need any time; let's get on with it." Then I glanced down at Dugin, lying on his side, looking up at me. He seemed so alone, so frightened. "I'll just take a few moments," I told the doctor.

I plunked myself down on a chair beside the table. Somehow, Dugin pushed his bloated body toward me and turned his head so he was now facing me. I patted him a few times and then languidly stroked his soft mane, mumbling that we all loved him and would miss him, and that he would go to a better place.

I didn't want to stop, knowing that by doing so I would be bringing his life to an end. Finally, and reluctantly, I called for Dr. Nelson. He came in and picked up the syringe and inserted the needle into a vein in Dugin's leg.

Now I was stroking him with both hands. He moaned once and then whimpered, his eyes sad and glassy, and, I felt, fully aware of what was about to happen. Dr. Nelson looked over at me. I nodded quickly, knowing if I didn't, I would lose my resolve. The doctor slowly pushed the plunger down, releasing the liquid. Moments later, Dugin's body heaved one last time and his eyes closed. At least he won't suffer anymore. I wonder if we can say the same about Dad.

DR. TREMBLAY
DAY 261—AN UPDATE

It's been a while since I have given you an update on Mr. Reimer. Unfortunately, but predictably, the news isn't very good. It's been less than a year since Mrs. Reimer called me to inform me she was having her husband admitted to Manoir Laurier. Frankly, I thought she should have done it long before, for both their sakes, but the pattern seems to be for a caregiver-spouse to go through torment, agony, and especially guilt, until he or she can't take it anymore. I believe that's what happened to Mrs. Reimer in this case.

I've been to see Mr. Reimer several times in the last few months at Manoir Laurier. His case is fairly typical, the timing of each stage approximating the median. I would have to say he is in the late stage of the disease now. That doesn't mean he will die in the next weeks or even months, but his cognitive and physiological abilities will continue to deteriorate at an even more rapid pace, until his entire system shuts down.

One thing we really don't know empirically is how much, if anything, patients at this stage can comprehend. We do know that their ability to communicate coherently is practically nil. Sometimes a slight gesture, eye movement, or facial expression may be conveying any thoughts they may have. Occasionally, for a brief moment or moments, for some reason especially near the end, they may appear lucid and say a few words. Whether this is by rote or an actual mental decision, we don't know at this point.

A wince may mean they're in pain, and then we have to do tests to discover what, if any, other medical problem they may have that might be causing them discomfort.

There are two existing tools used to identify the severity of dementia, the Reisberg Scale, I've alluded to previously, and the Functional Assessment Staging. Both have shown communication abilities in individuals with late-stage Alzheimer's disease to be minimal to nonexistent. There's a fine line between the two. The former means there is at least some comprehension, even, if as stated, it is minimal. The question is, Can they really make any sense of it, and if, so how much? So far, there has been no conclusive research on this subject that I am aware of.

Yesterday, I told Mrs. Reimer that her husband would be better off on the third floor where there is more supervision. At first, she was adamant that he stay where he was, but I could see through her tears that she really wasn't in a state of denial, but just was having trouble coping with the cruelness of it all. I assured her it was best for Mr. Reimer.

She looked up at me, patted my arm, and said, "I know, I know."

MONIQUE
DAY 430—A STEP CLOSER

Today is a day that I've thought about for a long time but prayed would never happen, even though Dr. Tremblay suggested it months ago. Saul is finally being moved from his room on the fourth floor down to the third. As I think I mentioned a while back, the third floor is reserved for those with . . . those who are the . . . what I'm trying to say is it's the floor for the ones I used to call the zombies. You probably remember my referring to them that way when Saul first got here. Well, now he's one of them, one of those who are incapable of almost any normal functions, physical or mental.

The move was scheduled for two o'clock. We had a family discussion and decided it would be less disruptive if we moved the furniture and his belongings while he was downstairs at the sing-along—not that he sings anymore. That way, hopefully, he wouldn't really notice and become more confused than he already is.

The room is almost the same size, although the windows are on the left side instead of the right. Apart from that, and the walls being green, with his furniture and paintings, it should look almost the same. This is one time when I hope he won't notice anything.

Now it's five o'clock, and they haven't moved a thing. The men who were supposed to do it were held up in traffic due to the snowstorm. I can't blame them for that, but meanwhile we had already packed up the room on the fourth floor, and here we are in Saul's new room on the third floor with bare walls and no furniture except a stool I took from the corridor and Saul's wheelchair. It seems so lonely and cold.

So far, Saul doesn't look like he notices anything different. At least I don't think so. But he's making some of the strange noises he sometimes makes when he gets agitated, so maybe he does.

But to be honest, I think the whole thing is affecting me more than him. To be alone, just the two of us, in this empty room, unable to communicate . . . Oh my God, I would give anything to turn back the clock.

SAUL

DAY 430—WHERE?

NOWhere noThiNg

MONIQUE
DAY 551—A MODERN-DAY TORTURE CHAMBER

I went to a movie last night. It was a beautiful evening, so afterward I decided to walk over to Manoir Laurier. It was about nine o'clock when I exited the elevator and approached the open door to Saul's room. I heard hysterical howling interspersed with a barrage of swearing. A nurse, with an unlit cigarette and a lighter tucked in her hand, walked by the room, not bothering to look in, and turned right toward a small balcony off the end of the corridor.

What I saw when I got inside Saul's room is almost beyond description. There he was, flailing away, trying to escape the restraints wrapped around his body. There were ropes strung through the sidebars, pinning down his legs, hips, and chest, so only his head could move. His face was a flushed crimson as he struggled to get up. He was like a madman, his words barely intelligible, his shrill ranting piercing the air, his head bobbing up and down. What in God's name were they doing to him? What did he ever do to anyone to deserve this kind of treatment?

I was able to loosen one of the ropes that bit into his hips and was working on the one that shackled his chest, when his head came up from nowhere and butted me in the forehead. I fell to the floor, my face covered in blood. Saul peered through the bars—trying to figure out what was going on, I guess.

It might have been the sight of the blood that precipitated what happened next. He went totally crazy. Now, half-freed from the restraints, he shook the bed, causing it to rock from side to side in such a way that I was sure it would collapse on me. He was like an animal, guttural sounds emanating from his contorted mouth as his eyes bulged.

Finally, he broke through the last restraint. It was like one of those Tarzan movies, where Tarzan would beat his chest before sliding down a vine.

As he looked down at me, I wasn't sure if he was about to kill me or save me. I guess I'll never know, because the nurse, who had seemed disinterested before she had her nicotine fix, rushed into the room. She pushed a panic button on the wall, then just stood there transfixed, not sure if she should help me or try to hold Saul back. She didn't have to make that decision, as within seconds four attendants swarmed into the room, pulling Saul to one side and me to the other. I sobbed as the nurse gave him a shot of something while the others held him. Seconds later, they lifted my slouching husband back on the bed and started to tie the restraints again.

I pushed one of the attendants aside. "Don't do that to him," I shrieked. "He's a human being, not an animal. Leave him alone."

I must have scared the devil out of them with that outburst, because they stopped in their tracks and looked over at me.

The bulky one with a shaved head said they were doing it for his own good, and so that what had happened to me wouldn't happen again.

I said, "What about drugs? Wouldn't they accomplish the same result?"

He just shrugged.

Later, I went to see the night administrator. She told me sometimes, as in Saul's case, when patients are extremely agitated, they have to use restraints so that the patients won't hurt themselves. Then with a pacifying smile, she said that as Saul's disease progresses, he will become more docile and will not need to be restrained. Did she think that would make me feel better?

SAUL
DAY 556—WHERE'S THE DOG?

thE DugiN cOme

MONIQUE
DAY 584—CONFUSION

As I awoke from another fitful sleep this morning, I reached over to Saul's side of the bed and felt the cold starched sheet, and, of course, no Saul. It's been ages now, and I still can't get used to it. I know it's forever and that he'll never come back. That he'll deteriorate in that damn pseudo hospital, while I rot here in what was our home for so many years.

Suzanne Latraverse, an acquaintance from the YMCA, has been pushing me to get on with my life and get out of the house—and maybe have some male companionship. She said it was more than enough to visit Saul every day, especially since he doesn't know me most of the time. As much as I might want to, I could never do it. Besides, I cannot understand who would want to spend any time with someone who is on the wrong side of seventy. So I must say I was more than surprised when Michael Salomon, one of our neighbors on Oakland Avenue, stopped me a few days ago as I passed his house on my way to see Saul.

Michael has been a widower for about five years now. We were friends with him and Bessie before she got her cancer. It seemed she was gone less than a month after they found it. In my opinion, she was lucky to go so fast.

Michael is a decent man, an ophthalmologist with his own practice. And not bad-looking. A bit heavy, but who am I to talk? He asked about Saul. The day before had been one of Saul's worst days. So I blurted out, "How terrible it is for both of us, this whole Alzheimer's thing."

He offered a cringing smile and then asked if I would like to have dinner one night. I think I babbled something like "Maybe" or "I'll see," something lame like that. He said he'd call me.

When I told Suzanne, she said I owed it to myself to go. But I wasn't sure I saw it that way. I felt disloyal even thinking of maybe having a good time while Saul was wasting away. Suzanne said, first of all, he wouldn't know. I countered that one could say the same about someone who cheats on her spouse behind his back. Then she said that maybe if I got out more, it would make me a better caregiver, calmer and less agitated. I wanted so much to see it her way, to get out of this goddamn house and go somewhere besides Manoir Laurier.

Michael called me the next day about dinner. I asked if he would call me back in an hour. After spending the hour scratching the rash that always seems to appear when I get nervous, I reluctantly agreed to go.

When we arrived at the restaurant, the young hostess showed us to a table by the window. Guess who was at the next table? Molly Kaplan, Westmount's unofficial gossip queen. I could feel her glaring at me as Michael put his hand on my elbow, slowing me so we could say hello. Molly was with Rachael Lipman, a shrew if ever there was one. I wanted so to twitch my nose and disappear like Samantha on *Bewitched*. I had a feeling they knew it and were relishing the whole thing.

The hostess seated us at the next table. I wanted to move, but I figured they would think they had caught us doing something immoral. It was the longest meal of my life.

Michael drove us back to Oakland Avenue and pulled into his driveway. I didn't protest, but a feeling of angst gripped me as he came around to open my door. It was all I could do to get out of the car. But mercifully, he led me past his house and directly to my front door. I put the key in the lock and barely turned around to thank him. It was eleven o'clock. I didn't sleep the whole night.

The phone rang at nine the next morning. It was Michael. He asked me to come over to watch a movie that night. I found myself quickly accepting, while at the same time wondering why. I, of course, knew the answer. I am practically a widow—God, I hate that word—lonely, sad, and desperate for company. As I showered before going to see Saul, a wave of guilt practically buckled my knees. How could I do this? How could I betray Saul? But I did go, and not only that, I had a good time—until Michael tried to kiss me good night. What was he thinking, for Christ's sake? I may be in a one-way relationship, but I'm still married. Or am I?

JOEY
DAY 589—GOING, GOING, GONE

I went to see Dad today. He was sitting in his wheelchair, his hands curled up, his head tilted to the side. I gave him my "Yo, Pops" greeting, but he didn't budge.

I looked down at him, his neck slouching against his chest, his lower lids bulging out, seemingly propping up his closed eyes. For the first time, it really hit me. He's a dead man. Maybe not officially, but a dead man nonetheless.

Jesus Christ! How could that have happened so quickly? Well, in retrospect, I guess it wasn't so fast. He's been in that place for almost two years.

I remember when he first got there, he was so much better than the others that I just figured it would always be like that. Now he's one of them. Well, maybe not. Because my best guess is the ones who were like he is today are probably six feet under.

I leaned over him and whispered in his ear. "Pops, I know you think I'm a zippo. I can't help what you believe. But let me assure you that I can take care of everything. I'm up to it. I really am. Just let go. I don't know if you're suffering, but even if you're not, this can't be any picnic. So why don't you just give it up and go. I'll take care of Mom and Florence."

He didn't open his eyes or give me any indication he'd heard me. But that wouldn't be surprising, even if he weren't sick. He's always figured he's the only one who can handle anything. It's like he's the last man who can make sense of this world.

"Well, Pops," I said, "I hate to tell you, but that's not the way it is anymore, in case you haven't noticed. So just give it up for everybody's sake—Mom's, Florence's, yours—and yeah, mine, too. We don't want to keep coming here and seeing you like this. We want to remember you the way you were.

"Do you recall how pissed we all were that your friend Christopher Rymond never once came to see you after you got sick? No, I guess you don't. Well, I bumped into him at a restaurant last week, and you know what he told me? He said he hadn't been around to see you because he wanted to remember you the way you were, not the way you most surely are now.

"I feel the same. But I have no choice. You're my father. So I show up. Maybe not often, but as much as I can, given how pissed I am about the state you're in. Anyway, it's really tough watching you like this. So please, put all of us out of our misery. Please!"

MONIQUE
DAY 624—OUR FIFTIETH

Today was our fiftieth anniversary. Not quite what I envisioned when I walked down the aisle. Well, at least we got this far, which is more than a lot of people.

Saul was too far gone to remember the date. In fact, he couldn't even understand what a wedding anniversary is. Nonetheless, that didn't stop me from inviting the family over to room 315 at Manoir Laurier for a celebration. Don't ask me why I did it. I know it sounds dumb. But I felt if I didn't, I would be betraying, or maybe the right word is *belittling*, our union. And besides, what could be the downside? I've given up caring what people think. It's too late for that.

Florence made a cake with two candles on it. The pink words on the icing just said *Monique and Saul, Fifty Years*. We all sat around—well, Florence and Bernie, Joey and I. Florence decided that she just couldn't bring the kids around anymore. She said it was giving them nightmares. And I don't blame her. I'm immune to it all now, and besides, I have to be there. But they don't, and I agree with her decision.

I got there early and helped the attendant dress Saul. I wasn't going to make him wear a suit and parade him around, but I did want to make sure he had on a clean shirt and sweater.

Once he was dressed, I tied the plastic bib around his neck and began to feed him. It's a long and tedious process because he doesn't eat on his own anymore and hasn't for months. Just getting him to open his mouth and swallow—well, it can take forever. At least he doesn't have solid foods anymore, so we don't have to worry about him choking.

I usually get there to give him lunch and go back around five o'clock to feed him dinner. On the days that I can't or don't, Florence goes instead.

By the time the others arrived, Saul was sleeping again. I gently shook him, and he slowly opened his eyes. I went over and sat beside him, taking his hand in mine. Florence lit the candles and held the cake in front of us. Bernie snapped a few photos with his new camera. I said, "Come on, Saul, we'll each blow out a candle." But he didn't respond. So I blew out the two candles and with that, I felt, what was left of our marriage.

FLORENCE
DAY 640—WHAT NEXT?

We were at Manoir Laurier this morning, Mother, Bernie, and I. Father was having one of his good days. Everything's relative, but his eyes were open and they seemed to be following at least some of our conversation. Mother was complaining about Joey and how he hadn't been there all week. So what else is new? She said she wouldn't prompt him to visit anymore. That if he didn't care, there was nothing more she could do.

Bernie defended Joey, saying that he just might not be able to cope with all of this. Mother got red in the face and started yelling at no one in particular. Venting, really. She said it has been hell for her but that she shows up. That she probably coddled Joey too much when he was young, and now he has no sense of responsibility. He doesn't think about anyone but himself and is driven only by money.

Father looked at her like he was in agreement, his head nodding slightly as he kept her in his gaze. That seemed to spur her on. She shifted her focus to Father, talking to him like he could understand her, asking him where they went wrong. Almost like she was actually expecting an answer. Father uttered a few incoherent words, while Mother persisted, her voice shaking.

Suddenly, she pulled her hands to her chest. Her eyes widened. Her breathing accelerated. She fell back in her chair. I asked her what was wrong. She said she felt dizzy and had pain in her back. I could see perspiration on her forehead. Bernie said he would ring for the nurse.

Mother shook her head, saying it would pass in a few seconds. She closed her eyes for a moment, then raised herself up in her chair and looked over at Father. He just stared at her, mumbling. She got only a few more words out before her eyes glazed over. I screamed for Bernie to press the emergency button, and then I grabbed Mother's purse, dumping the contents on the floor until her nitro pump fell out.

I administered it while Bernie called 911 on his cell phone. The nurses got there in a few seconds, and minutes later the medics arrived. After tending to Mother, they placed her on a stretcher and wheeled her down the hall toward the elevator and out to the ambulance.

MONIQUE
DAY 651—A CLOSE CALL

I've spent eleven days sharing a room with three other people in the hospital. If I weren't already sick, this would do it. I don't think I've gotten more than an hour's sleep any night. The man next to me has a raspy cough that sounds like he is in the throes of death. The man in the cubicle opposite me is Spanish or Mexican and has a loud extended family that pours in at all hours, even though the night nurse has read them the riot act.

And then there was the poor woman in the cubicle on my right. She was only thirty-nine, and from Haiti. She had just brought her two daughters to Canada after a period of three years, when they had to stay with their grandmother down there while their visa applications went through Canada's bureaucratic process. They were barely teenagers and so well behaved. I wish mine had been like that when they were those girls' ages. Well, I guess Florence was pretty good.

Speaking of Florence, I told her not to visit me and to spend time with her father instead. But you know her—she spends lunch and dinner with him and then comes to see me at night.

The third morning, just after sunrise, they came to prepare the Haitian woman for surgery. She gave me a tight smile as they wheeled her away. I could tell by her eyes that she was frightened—and who wouldn't be.

I followed the slow-moving hands of the clock beside the window all day. By dinnertime, she still hadn't returned. Around nine that night, they rolled an elderly man into her cubicle. The woman from Haiti had died on the operating table. I told the nurse to get the number for her daughters. I will send a check to them at their aunt's house. And then when I'm better, I'll go see them.

I must say as bad as the conditions are in the hospital, the doctors are fantastic. They told me that I was close to death when I arrived at the emergency room, that I had arrhythmia and my heart had actually stopped at Manoir Laurier. They said the medics had used a defibrillator and administered some medications. The nurse told me what they were, but they all had such long names, I can't remember them. She said when I arrived at the hospital, they had inflated a balloon in the arteries around my heart and cleared three blockages. They said I would have been released earlier, but I had some complications. I'm getting some other medications now, and they seem to be working, because I feel a little stronger. The doctor in charge of the ward said I should be able to go home tomorrow—not a day too soon.

JOEY
DAY 651—FINALLY, A GOOD DREAM

I can't remember a night that I haven't had terrible dreams—actually, horrible nightmares. Last night was different. I had my usual glass of chardonnay and a few tokes of weed before I turned off the light and fell asleep.

Here, to the best of my recollection, is what I dreamed: Dad was sitting at the foot of my bed, dressed in a blue suit, white dress shirt, and red tie. His posture was straight, like he had a steel rod in his back. His face was serene, his smile calm. He told me that I was a better son to him than he was to his father. That our conflicts were not my fault, but, rather, a result of his being stubborn and obstinate. He apologized for the tantrums, the doubts, and his lack of emotional involvement. He said he loved me and only wanted my happiness. Then he stood up, leaned over, and hugged me. I could feel the wet tears falling off his face onto my cheek. They were warm and cold at the same time. More important, they were comforting. He stayed in that position for a long time, seemingly not wanting to stop. And frankly, I didn't want him to, either.

I generally remember only fragments of my nightmares, just enough to haunt me. But this morning when I woke up, every gesture, every word, every movement of last night's dream was so vivid, like it actually happened. If only it had.

FLORENCE
DAY 656—A MIRACLE

Last Sunday, I was at Mother's house, preparing for her return home. It's ironic that she had moved the bedroom downstairs for Father, and now it is she who can't climb the stairs.

She was at the hospital for over ten days after the attack. The cardiologist told me her heart is really diseased, and the prognosis for some kind of normal life will depend a lot on her stress level.

Mother insisted that she didn't want a caretaker living in her house. I can certainly understand that. Who wants a stranger living in your house 24/7. I told her I would take a leave of absence from my work and move in until she was strong enough to manage for herself. I have cut back my hours a lot since having the kids anyway, and even more so since Father got sick. The partners at the firm have been very understanding. As long as I take care of my clients, they have no problem with my working on my files at home.

Bernie wasn't happy that I'd be staying with Mother, but he understood. The kids said they would come by every day after school, do their homework, and stay for dinner, so at least we could see one another.

Bernie went to pick up Mother while I left to get some groceries. I chose things I knew she might not like but that were good for her. I realized that wasn't going to go over well, but I certainly wasn't going to contribute to another heart attack.

When they arrived, I helped her into the house and into her room. She had begun light exercise, walking the corridors of the hospital, but she was still very weak.

I got her undressed, put her in bed, and went into the kitchen to prepare dinner.

Only minutes after Bernie left to get back to the children, the doorbell rang. I wasn't expecting anyone at five o'clock on a Sunday afternoon. I wiped my hands on the kitchen towel by the stove and walked through the living room to the front door.

I almost keeled over when I opened it. Joey was standing there with a suitcase in his hand. He looked like a door-to-door salesman carrying his wares. I asked him what he was doing there. What he said almost gave *me* a heart attack. After everything I've told you about him, you couldn't imagine his answer. He said he was moving in with Mother and would take care of her. That I could go home to my children. That he would stay with her until she was better.

JOEY

DAY 660—WHY MOVE IN WITH MOM?

That's a good question. One I've been asking myself over and over. If I had to rank my parents in order, I'm not sure exactly how it would come out; maybe neither of them would make the top spot. Like I've said before, in their own way they probably did what they could. And I guess they learned their parenting skills from their parents, so you can't really blame them. But nonetheless, I still had to endure my father's icy demeanor. I mean, how many fathers, when at seven years old you go to kiss them good night, would offer you a handshake instead—and never kiss you again? And my mother's being preoccupied with her favorite Florence all the time. What about me?

Anyway, what's done is done, and here I am. I realize that no parent is perfect, despite what we thought when we were kids. And so to compensate for some of the things that go missing in our childhood, we tend to go one way or the other. I'm having trouble saying this clearly, but what I mean is that Florence is the way she is because of how she was treated as a kid, and the same goes for me.

In spite of everything, seeing Mom lying there so close to death really scared me and made me realize how mortal we all are. Especially me, now that I have the ApoE4 genes. I'd want to know someone would be there for me if something were to happen.

I told Florence I would stay with Mom until she's better, figuring it will be a month—tops. Even I can handle that. But frankly, if it stretches on much longer than that, then I'll have to reassess the whole thing.

FLORENCE
DAY 668—THE VISIT

I pulled my Volvo into Mother's driveway just before noon. A minute later, she appeared on Joey's arm from the side door. Her hair was up in a bouffant. She had on Father's favorite dress, the blue one with the silver stripes on the sleeves. Given she had been back home for just over two weeks, it wasn't surprising that she looked tired. Her gait was a bit wobbly, but Joey held on to her elbow to steady her as she got into the front seat. This would be the first time she would see Father since her heart attack.

When we walked into Father's room, he was staring at the television, seemingly in a trance.

But a moment later, he turned toward Mother and said, "*Bonjour, chou-fleur.*"

I had to hold on to her, as I thought she would collapse right there.

She reached out for his hand and stroked it. "*Bonjour, mon cher,*" she said.

Father smiled and put his hand on top of hers. If I hadn't been there to see it myself, I never would have believed it.

I slid a chair under her, and Joey helped her into it. Her hand didn't move, and neither did Father's. They just looked into each other's eyes, their gazes never moving, transfixed, experiencing something we weren't privy to. Seconds later, Father's vacuous stare returned to the television, and the moment ended.

Joey said, "Mom, he knows you're here."

Mother nodded, and said, "Yes, I'm sure he does."

And I believe he did. He has those moments where you just know he's back with you. This was definitely one of them.

Twenty minutes later, Joey looked at his watch and cleared his throat. Mother and I were familiar with the signal. It was time to go. I helped her up. She bent over Father and gave him a kiss on his forehead, followed by a kiss on his lips, and a long hug. Then she took Joey's arm, and we left Father's room.

MONIQUE
DAY 668—MY SAUL

Joey, Florence, and I went down to visit Saul today. Maybe I'm just getting used to seeing him like that, shriveled, hands closed, like he's holding one of Dugin's balls, his face contorting now and then. So when I first saw him today, it was not any different from any other day.

Then he looked at me. I mean really looked at me. It was as if we were connecting once again, just like when we first met. I don't believe it lasted for more than a minute, if that, but it was truly magic.

I don't remember if he said anything besides when he called me *chou-fleur*. That stunned me. Other than nonsensical chatter, he hasn't uttered a word in over a year. It was as if he felt this might be the last time we would ever see each other. And, you know, I think it was so powerful for both of us, that even if it were the last time, what a wonderful way for me to remember him.

Dr. Tremblay said that Alzheimer's patients sometimes open their eyes like they're trying to communicate, wanting to say good-bye, just before they pass away. I always thought that was hogwash. If they can't think, how could they do that? Yet I am convinced that's what happened today. And that's going to both comfort me and cause me anguish as I try to sleep tonight.

SAUL

DAY 668—I SAW HER

JuSt . . . hEr as Pretti . . . CHoo fLeuR

JOEY
DAY 669—TOO SOON

Around seven this morning, I took Mom some tea and dry toast. I placed the tray on the dresser by her bed. She was lying on her side, facing the wall. I said, "Mom, time for breakfast." No reply. I said again, "Mom, your breakfast is here." Nothing. So I shook her a little, not wanting to startle her. She rolled over, away from me just a bit, but enough to alarm me. I took her by the shoulders and tried to move her into a sitting position, but she was limp. I felt her face. It was cold. I don't know how to take someone's pulse, but it was clear to me that she was gone.

Before bedtime, she had complained about having the worst headache of her life. I gave her two Tylenol and stayed with her until she fell asleep. I looked in on her around midnight and could hear her moving in the darkness, so it must have happened between then and seven. Anyway, I called 911, and the medics were here within minutes. I watched as the younger one felt for a pulse. After a moment, he looked up at me and shook his head.

To be honest with you, I didn't know what I would feel when Mom died. We were never that close. But it really hit me when the guy looked up at me. I watched her lying there alone in that big bed, no one to hold her, no one to protect her. I guess it's too late for all that.

Do you remember I told you before that I would stay with her for up to a month and then reassess the situation if she wasn't better? Well, I meant it then, but as the time went by, I realized for the first time how much she loved me, and how just opening myself up a little to her, exposing myself a bit, just taking a chance—how much better it made me feel.

I actually realized it a few days after she got back from the hospital. I had made her a sandwich for lunch and called her into the kitchen. She shuffled in from the living room in her worn pink slippers, which she must have had since before my bar mitzvah. Her body wavered from side to side. I reached out and took her arm, guiding her to the chair by the window.

She looked up at me and said, "Joey, you have been out of my life for too long."

I knew she was right, and it wasn't proximity she was referring to. It was an emotional distance that had stretched further and further as time went on—until now. Sadly, with that epiphany less than a couple of weeks old, she's gone.

And now I feel like I'm rootless. Florence has Bernie and the kids. Even Dad has the staff at the home, although whether he even knows that is another story. But when I leave here today and go back to the apartment, I'll basically be an orphan. I have no real attachments to my sister or her family. I can't even remember the last time I went over when it was just us being together and not a family meeting about Dad. Sure, I've got some friends, but no one who would go to the mat for me, and as for girlfriends—maybe I should have kept Maria or even Gabrielle. But that all doesn't matter now. They're gone from my life, and there are no replacements on the horizon.

So here I am. Alone. No mother. No father. No one.

FLORENCE
DAY 669—SHOCK

I usually don't drink, but last night Bernie and I celebrated our wedding anniversary at the local bistro with a bottle of champagne. So this morning when the phone rang, I just let it go to voice mail. Less than a minute later, it rang again. Daniel must have been up, playing one of his video games, and he answered. I heard him yell for me, so I fumbled for the phone, dragging the cord toward me.

When I finally got the receiver close to my ear, I heard Joey on the other end. He stumbled and stuttered, but finally he was able to give me the news. I won't say I was totally surprised. Mother did look somewhat pallid and unstable on her feet yesterday. But still, you don't think of a parent dying so suddenly. It's different when you're prepared, like we probably will be with Father when his time comes.

I rushed over to the house. Joey answered the door. I could see a medic standing in the doorway; he was on his cell phone. I asked him if he could leave me alone with Mother for a few minutes. Then I walked through the open door, sat on the bed, and pulled her close to me. She was cold and pale and moist. I held her tightly against my chest. Somehow, I couldn't cry. I think I felt that by crying I would be acknowledging her passing, and I wasn't ready to do that—not yet anyway.

I talked to her like I often do with Father, his eyes closed, his body limp except for the odd twitch. I have often wondered if he hears me, but you know what? I don't do it for him, and wasn't doing it for Mother now. I was doing it for me, to bring me closer.

FLORENCE
DAY 671—MOTHER'S FUNERAL

This isn't the way it was supposed to happen. Father was the one who would go first, even though Mother had a bad heart. That's what we've all thought for the longest time. The doctor reassured us that she probably died quickly and without pain. Thank God for that.

Now here we are in the mourners' area in the sanctuary at Silverberg and Sons, waiting for the last few people to take their seats. The place looks about three-quarters full.

From here, I can see Nicole Drapkin, one of my classmates at McGill. The handsome man beside her must be her new husband. And there's Jamie Ram. I can't believe he came. I haven't seen him for at least twenty years. I used to have a crush on him back in high school, before I met Bernie. And there are several more people I never would have guessed would have bothered to show up. I can even see a couple of Joey's old girlfriends toward the back. It's funny how death sometimes spawns renewed friendships. Maybe that's God's way of compensating the next of kin for their loss.

Mother's casket is sitting below the lectern, from which I'll be giving a eulogy after the one by Rabbi Phillips. I really hope I can hold it together and not break down. That's going to be hard to do, given my emotional state. So I'll just try to block out the people and read my notes.

I asked Joey if he wanted to say anything. He said I could say it best. And I guess he's right. That's probably because I spent more time with Mother. Although I'm sure Joey's turnaround in going to stay with her before she passed away brought them closer.

Father is sitting beside me in his wheelchair. Joey and I had a heated discussion as to whether he should come. Joey was afraid his appearance might embarrass us. I told him that was ridiculous. First of all, everyone here knows about Father's condition. But putting that aside, the important thing is what Mother would have wanted. I know she would have wanted him here, and I know Father wouldn't have it any other way, if he could voice his opinion.

Father's eyes seem to open every few seconds, look at the casket, then close again. It's like he's doing whatever he can to focus, that he knows what's happening. And who knows, maybe he does. Well, the rabbi is about to deliver his eulogy . . .

JOEY
DAY 671—MOM'S FUNERAL

I think it was a mistake for Dad to be here. What was Florence thinking? I told her he wasn't in any condition to come to the funeral. And once again, I was right. It started off okay, with him sitting between us. But when the rabbi finished his eulogy and Florence stood up, Dad started wailing. I couldn't figure out whether he wasn't with the program and just howling, or if he truly knew what was happening and was grieving. Either way, it took Florence and me what seemed like an eternity, but was probably only a couple of minutes, to calm him down so that Florence could move to the lectern.

I must admit she was very eloquent and probably right about Mom and Dad's relationship, at least the part she talked about. She didn't get into their constant bickering, but I guess you don't do dirty laundry at funerals.

She did, however, talk about their devotion to each other, and how Mom loved us, bragging to her friends all the time about what great children we were. I could see a few of her friends in the front pews nodding in agreement. That's all very nice, but it would have been better had she—and Dad—told us instead of their friends, if, indeed, Dad did feel that way. And that's something I guess I will never know for sure, given the state he's in now.

SAUL

DAY 671—MONIQUE'S FUNERAL

Whatt's the BoX? why sha's nOt herre?

DR. TREMBLAY
DAY 678—THE REIMERS

I have just returned to my office after having spent the morning at Manoir Laurier. During that time, I visited Mr. Reimer's room to check up on him. His son and daughter were there. I offered my condolences on their mother's passing last week. I have seen the daughter quite a bit during my visits, but I haven't seen the son—Joey, I believe is his name—since he came to me a few years ago about his ApoE genes.

To be frank with you, Mrs. Reimer's passing didn't come as a great surprise. I had seen her several times since her husband was diagnosed. It's been probably a little more than six years now, to the best of my memory, but without the file in front of me, I can't be exactly sure. She appeared to be a strong woman, certainly stronger than most spouses I encounter. But with her heart condition and unwillingness to allow Mr. Reimer to spend a few hours a day at the Schaffer Centre so she could get some well-deserved time off, coupled with her adamant refusal to join any caregiver support groups—well, in my mind, it could not really have ended much differently.

Mr. Reimer is definitely in the last stage of the disease. His reflexes are almost nonexistent, his muscles completely rigid now, and his swallowing quite labored. As I stated before, he may comprehend the odd snippet of conversation, but that's something that we'll never know, given his inability to communicate logically at this point.

I checked the chart while I was there, and the "Do not resuscitate" and "No heroic measures" orders were still there. Since the children were present, I wanted to get a quick confirmation that this was still their choice. Both the daughter and her brother reaffirmed their decision. That's the hardest part of my practice, watching the suffering the family goes through toward the end. But I believe it's coupled with relief, both for themselves and the patient, that it's almost over.

FLORENCE
DAY 685—IT'S TIME

It's been two weeks since Mother's funeral. Even though we're Jewish, I would say we're probably more culturally Jewish than religious. *Shiva* lasted only two days, instead of the customary seven. If you're unfamiliar with the practice of sitting *shiva,* it's a mourning period when the immediate family receives condolences at home, and when friends and family gather for prayers.

Part of the reason we cut it short is that I can't leave Father alone for too long because of his condition, which, incidentally, has deteriorated since Mother died. If it didn't fly in the face of logic, I would swear he knows exactly what happened.

Regardless, he is really in bad shape now. Bad enough that as much as I hated Joey for repeating over the last few months that he hoped Father would die, that's how I feel now.

I am absolutely drained from all this. It's not about me, and if it meant my rearranging everything to spend more time with Father, I gladly would. But I just can't stand to see him in that condition, especially with no possibility of ever getting better. No, it's time— time for Father to stop suffering, and time for what's left of our family to move on.

I'm worried about Joey. I can't remember the last instance we spent time together. My children hardly know him. Sometimes I wonder if I even know him.

He pretends he's a man of the world, with his new business and all his girlfriends, but I think inside he's a frightened child. After he saw Dr. Tremblay and found out about his having two copies of that ApoE4 gene, you would think he would have voiced some concern. But aside from when he came to see me to break the news, he hasn't mentioned it again. And when I brought it up a few times, he just made light of it.

He has told me in the past that he is the way he is because of his upbringing. Maybe that's true, maybe not. But all that doesn't matter anymore. We are where we are in life, and it won't do any good to place blame, if indeed there is any blame to place.

JOEY
DAY 690—THE LETTER

Yesterday, Florence, Bernie, and I went over to the house on Oakland. We decided that we might as well as go through Mom and Dad's stuff, since no one will be living there anymore—at least no one from our family.

While going through Mom's desk, I came across a copy of her and Dad's wills, as well as their living mandates. Now, Dad isn't gone yet, but, given his condition, I figured it wouldn't hurt to read everything. Florence and Bernie agreed.

The bottom line is, Dad's will leaves everything to Mom. Her will leaves everything to Dad. And there is a provision in both wills stating that Florence and I should share what's left once they're both gone. The living mandates give Florence and me power of attorney. Florence said we probably should sell the house. Sounds good to me. I could finally pay off my debts, including the thirty-plus grand I owe Bernie.

They asked me what I wanted besides my share of the house. I said I'd like the family photo that Mom kept by the side of her bed. And that's all I really wanted—honest. I'm not saying if there was something of great value that I wouldn't have asked for my part.

As we went through Mom's desk, Florence came across two letters. The front of one envelope said, *For Joey, to be opened after my death.* The other one was for Florence. They were from Dad. I could tell by the shaky handwriting.

I stuffed my envelope inside my jacket. I certainly wasn't going to open it in front of them, especially after Florence said maybe we should wait till Dad dies before reading them. She said the letters were different from a will. But I didn't think I would be violating any trust, given Dad's condition.

Anyway, I went to see him this morning. I took the letter with me. Somehow, I felt if I read it in front of him—I don't know—maybe it would be more kosher. I guess it sounds stupid, but that's how I felt.

When I went into the room, he was in his chair beside the bed, facing the window that looks down on the garden. His eyes were shut tight, almost as if he were squinting.

I yelled out, "Yo, Pops," but got no response. Not that I was expecting any. I moved over to the bed and plopped myself down beside him. He didn't budge.

I hesitated for a moment, then reached into my pocket and pulled out the envelope and took a long, deep breath. As I tore it open and pulled out the single page, I said, "Pops, this better be good, or else!"

I began to read the scribbled writing: *Dear Joey, I never told you while I was alive how much I loved you and how proud I was . . .*

My body sank and I began to shake. I didn't know whether to be ecstatic or furious. He actually was proud of me. He even said he loved me. But why couldn't he say it to my face when he could think, when he could speak? He had forty years to utter just those few words—words that would have changed both our lives.

I looked over at him, hunched in his chair. Suddenly, his eyes opened and seemed to focus on me. He mumbled something. The only word I could make out was son. And I wasn't even 100 percent sure about that. What I was sure about was that his eyes were saying what his voice couldn't. I reached over to hug him. Then I opened up his clenched hand and squeezed. I swear I could feel him press his palm against mine.

I don't know how much longer he has, but I won't miss a day from now on—not one!

MONTREAL *GAZETTE*
JANUARY 6, 2015

Reimer, Saul Nathaniel. Peacefully, in his seventy-seventh year, on Monday, January 5, 2015, at Manoir Laurier in Montreal. Beloved husband of the late Monique Proulx Reimer. Devoted father of Florence and Joey. Cherished brother of the late Miriam. Loving son of the late Lawrence and Hannah Reimer, and son-in-law of the late Sebastien and Carole Proulx. Caring father-in-law of Bernard Weiner. Adored grandfather of Howard and Daniel. He will be sadly missed by all his family and friends. We would like to express our sincere appreciation for the warmth and kindness shown him by the wonderful staff at Manoir Laurier. Funeral services will take place at Silverberg and Sons, Wednesday, January 7, at 2:00 p.m. Donations in his memory can be made to the Alzheimer's Society of Canada.

ACKNOWLEDGMENTS

I would once again like to thank Jim Wade, my editor, for his work on this novel. His perception and acumen is truly appreciated. In addition, I would like to acknowledge Carol Edwards, my copy editor, and a special thanks to Sharon Nettles, proofreader, editor, and all-around helper for her diligent work in making sure this novel made it to press on time and in good shape.

Dr. Serge Gauthier, director of the Alzheimer's Research Unit at McGill University, is one of the most respected researchers in the field. Without him, this book would not have been possible. He spent an enormous amount of time making sure my medical facts were correct and encouraged me to continue when the going was tough. Thank you, Serge!

And of course, Christine Schaffer, who read draft, after draft, after draft. If there were a prize for patience and understanding, she would be the clear winner.

To Chris Dymond, Kia Bossom Wood, Andrée Laganière, and Jim Brodsky—I thank you for your support.

And finally, a posthumous thank you to Jim Phillips and Mel Leeb, who were there for me every step of the way. I am so sorry you aren't here to see this book come to fruition. I miss you both.

ABOUT THE AUTHOR

I was born in Montreal and graduated from Cornell University with a bachelor of arts, and from UCLA with an MBA. Having held several executive positions in the hospitality industry, including president of a global hotel group, I finally figured out that I was more the creative type than the corporate type. So I packed up and headed to the Caribbean, where I wrote my first novel, *Pinnacle Of Deceit*. That was followed by *The Innocent Traitor*. My third novel was to be another thriller, but after I was more than halfway through, I put it aside and penned *An Absent Mind*, a novel I knew I had to write, having been through eight years with my father's Alzheimer's. My goal was not only to write good fiction, but also to provide readers with a true picture of this dreaded disease that afflicts more than 35 million people worldwide. I truly hope I was able to achieve that.